Factory Girl

Factory Girl

by Josanne La Valley

CLARION BOOKS 🐝 HOUGHTON MIFFLIN HARCOURT 🐝 BOSTON NEW YORK

CLARION BOOKS
3 Park Avenue, New York, New York 10016

Copyright © 2017 by Josanne La Valley

Clarion Books is an imprint of
Houghton Mifflin Harcourt Publishing Company.

www.hmhco.com

The text was set in Meridien LT Std.

Library of Congress Cataloging-in-Publication Data
Names: La Valley, Josanne.
Title: Factory girl / Josanne La Valley.
Description: Boston; New York: Clarion Books, Houghton Mifflin Harcourt,
[2017] I Summary: "In order to save her family's farm, Roshen,
sixteen, must leave her rural home to work in a factory in the south
of China. There she finds arduous and degrading conditions and contempt
for her minority (Uyghur) background. Sustained by her bond with
other Uyghur girls, Roshen is resolved to endure all to help her family
and ultimately her people"—Provided by publisher.
Identifiers: LCCN 2016001513 I ISBN 9780544699472 (hardback)
Subjects: LCSH: Uighur (Turkic people)—China—Juvenile fiction. I CYAC:
Uighur (Turkic people)—Fiction. I Factories—Fiction. I Work--Fiction.
I Prejudices—Fiction. I Ethnic relations—Fiction. I China—Fiction.
Classification: LCC PZ7.V2544 Fac 2017 I DDC [Fic]—dc23

Manufactured in the United States of America
DOC 10 9 8 7 6 5 4 3 2 1
4500632374

*To the Uyghur people of East Turkestan in their struggle
to preserve their language, culture, and religion
and to live freely in their own land.*

Uyghur *is pronounced WEEgur.*

Factory Girl

One

IT HAPPENS THE LAST DAY of school. A dictate. Delivered to me, personally, by my teacher. It will change my life.

I tell no one. I try to celebrate Meryam's wedding as if it is the happiest of times, and it is, for her. Now the three days of her wedding are coming to a close as the bridegroom's family and friends take the bride from her home to the home of her new husband.

As we come near, we hop from the donkey carts that have carried us and form a procession. Four attendants are in the lead, and I am one of them, leading the gathering past the policemen and cameraman who have been assigned to attend our ancient ritual—which is still allowed, though I'm certain that's only because it's good for the Chinese tourist website. I try to erase the intruders from my mind as my arms move gracefully in wide waves and my feet keep the pattern of our dance. We approach the opened gate of the silk maker's compound to the steady beat of the musicians, who now pluck louder and louder on the strings of their instruments while one finger-drums the taut leather of his *dap*.

A rush, and Meryam's brother, Ahmat, and three other male relatives break through our gathering. They carry

Meryam, crouched, her head covered, in the middle of a richly colored carpet that they hold by its four corners. A bonfire burns in front of the groom's home, and they whoosh her through the leaping flames to show how she will endure the hardships of married life.

I slip inside the house, where her mother and I will provide the familiar hands to help her slide from the carpet to her seat on the floor beside her new relatives. She is expected to cry, to be scared and unsure, but I hear giggles behind the thick white covering that she must keep over her while the musicians play and sing of how the new couple will never part.

At last the cloth is lifted. A female cousin of the bride dances. Then we spill out into the courtyard for the last rituals of the three-day celebration, during which Ahmat and I have been so busy catering to Meryam's needs that it has been easy for me to avoid being alone with him.

He heads toward me now. I pretend not to see him, and with my arms raised I slide in among the dancers. He follows. We will each dance alone. That is the Uyghur way. But we are dancing together, our arms, our feet intertwining, almost touching. We are one. I know that so truly.

I force myself to think only of the repeated *taah*-te-ta-*tah-tah* of the beat — over and over — until the high-pitched chant of my little sister, Aygul, breaks through.

"You will be next. You will be next," Aygul teases as she dances at our side. Her words are picked up by those around us, even though the others know that Ahmat and

I intend to continue our studies, so there is no plan for a wedding yet.

I lower my head to hide my pain as Ahmat slowly turns his arms and feet away and joins the other dancers.

There is laughter at our expense. We've been caught in our oneness. They must think I'm shy, for I don't look up.

How could I?

In a few days, I'll be gone. Sent away.

There'll be no more schooling. Courtship? Wedding? Those words are no longer meant for me. I've been given the *honor*, my teacher said, of working in a factory far away in southern China. The local cadre will come speak to Father. Wait until after Meryam's wedding, I pleaded, and the teacher agreed.

I dance my way to the edge of the crowded courtyard and slip inside the weaving room. Today there is more interest in dancing and eating than in the weaving of ikat. I stand among the idle looms and let my sorrow flow from my eyes.

If I refuse to go, they'll deny me my schooling. There will never be a wedding. They'll take away my registration card and refuse to issue me a marriage certificate. I have no life if I go—or if I stay.

Ahmat moves toward me, and I don't have time to stop my tears. "Roshen," he says, "it's a happy event. Meryam has dreamed of this day for years." He brushes my tears away with his fingers, letting his touch linger on my cheeks. Even as my heart races, I push his hand away. I must not allow it. But my fingers go to my face and touch the place where his have been, for I want to remember the feeling forever.

He smiles, and for the longest time we devour each other with our eyes. No one can deny us that. Then we dance again, alone but together in our Uyghur way.

I say nothing about my leaving.

It is near evening when Aygul comes to tell me we must go home. Grandfather has clapped and sung until his old bones will hardly hold him upright long enough to get to the donkey cart. I spend little time saying good-bye to Meryam, for I do not trust myself to show only the joy she deserves. Yet she will not let me go and insists on walking me to the cart. And soon we are an entourage, for Meryam's mother, her father, and Ahmat all walk out too, to say goodbye to my family.

When the beats from the drum and the last sounds of music fade from our hearing, Father turns to me.

"Are you certain you want to keep going to school, Roshen?" Father says, and Grandmother, Mother, and Aygul cluck their tongues and laugh.

I'm caught off-guard. I pretend shyness, covering my face with my hands, hoping the coming darkness hides my distress.

Father laughs and prods the donkey to a faster pace. For now, the happy mood of Meryam's wedding prevails.

I will speak to him tomorrow.

Two

SLEEP HAS COME and gone. I linger on the sleeping platform a moment, storing the memory of Aygul's warmth next to me. I want to cradle my sister in my arms. Hold her near me forever.

That's not to be.

When I'm finally allowed to return home, will Aygul want me to hold her? She'll be almost nine years old. Will she think herself too grown up?

I dress quietly and leave the house unseen. I pass our sheep pens, the chicken coop. I wander through our gardens and fields, verdant with vegetables, corn, and grains. We will do well at market this summer. I stop and gaze in awe at the stark beauty of our mulberry trees, silhouetted in the first soft light of day. There is majesty in the naked branches, stripped of almost all their leaves to feed the thousands of hungry silkworms from which the finest thread will be spun.

This picture, this memory of our land, I will store and take with me. I've worked in these fields. Helped to sow, cultivate, and harvest their bounty. The land brings my family a good life.

I kick at the ground, stirring up the parched, sandy soil that shows how near our farm lies to the great Taklamakan Desert. I must remember the smell of this dusty place, where every breath is mixed with a bit of sand blown in from the desert. What will it smell like in a factory city? Will there be a patch of earth to kick at?

"Why am I the one you picked to go?" I cry out. Safe to say this here, where no one can overhear and cart me off to detention for daring to ask such a question. They sometimes arrest women for such talk. More likely they'd fine Father an impossible sum of money or take our farm.

I try to unclench my fists, for I came here to collect memories, not to rage against a force I can't control.

"Allah, help me," I whisper. I am not good at prayers, not certain how to speak to God. I'm worried about what will happen when I return home in a year. Rumors about the girls who have been sent away disturb me—some of them never come back. Those who do are often thought to be impure and unworthy of a Uyghur husband. "Keep me one with my home and my people while I am away."

I dare not think of Ahmat. Will he wait for me? Father wants us to marry. He has no sons and hopes that Ahmat will take over the farm one day. Both our families have long agreed that our marriage would be a good idea. Ahmat is much more interested in his agricultural and water management training—and the mismanagement of resources by the Chinese—than in following his father's trade as a wood craftsman.

The pale, shrouded sun begins to rise through the morning mist. I hurry back to the house before Aygul is sent to find me.

My family already sits around the eating cloth. I fix tea and take my place beside Mother. They've been especially quiet since I removed my shoes and came to sit with them. They look at the ground. Mother bites her lip and tries not to smile. It's Aygul who blurts out, "We're having a visitor today, Roshen, and we have lots of work to do to get ready. So eat fast."

They clap and ooh and aah, and then I know. This is the day Ahmat's mother has chosen to visit my family. She'll bring a golden ring, and they'll talk about whether an engagement between Ahmat and me is a suitable match.

My heart flies to unite with Ahmat's. The commitment for us to be together forever is as it should be. My answer, my family's answer, would be yes, but when I lift my face to them, the clapping slows. Then stops.

I shake my head.

"The visitor who comes," I say, "is one we do not want to see today. Mother, you must go to the wood craftsman's house and say this is not a good time."

Three

IN MIDAFTERNOON the local government cadre arrives in a car, and he is not alone.

The cadre and the Chinese man who has come with him stand stiff and formal in their too-big suit jackets, watching Father make his way from the house to the road to greet them. The cadre halfheartedly returns the gestures and words of Father's *assalam alaykum*. The Chinese man flicks dust from his sleeve and looks around. He says something in Mandarin that I am too far away to hear clearly.

I keep watch from behind the half-open door of the house as the cadre, the Chinese man, and Father head toward the sheep pens. Soon they're walking through the fields, and finally they move out of sight among the mulberry trees.

"What's happening, Roshen?" Aygul asks as she and Mother and I go into the yard.

Mother and I exchange glances and tighten our lips. Neither of us could think of a good way to tell Aygul. Other Uyghur girls have been sent away when they turned sixteen—the cadres have their quotas to fill. But we never imagined I might be one of them. The people at school had encouraged me to be a teacher. They knew I had passed my tests and was ready to move into teacher training.

I go to Aygul and fold my arms around her as we stare into the distance.

"The cadre has come to make arrangements for me to do service to my country." I turn her around so we are face-to-face. The innocence I see scares me. I've coddled her when I should have been making her tough.

"I'm going away," I say, even then making the words sound fun, as if it were an adventure. My hands shake as I grasp her shoulders. "Aygul, listen carefully. I will be gone, far away, for at least a year. The Chinese need help in their factories and they've chosen me to go. But I'll be back! And you must make a promise to me."

Aygul's hands fly to cover her face as she tries to pull away. "It's not true. You can't go," she cries.

But it is true. I want to make her promise that she'll keep studying, that she'll try to be better at speaking and reading Mandarin than the Chinese themselves. They don't want us to speak our Uyghur language. Then I remember that I was best at Mandarin and English and everything else, and that did nothing to protect me. I have no words of wisdom or comfort to pass on to my sister.

We stand in silence as Father returns with the cadre and the Chinese man.

"Come inside, Roshen, and make tea for us," Father says, holding the door for the men to enter our home.

I soon understand why he didn't ask Mother to prepare the tea. The Chinese man speaks little Uyghur. Father wants me to listen and let him know if the cadre is translating correctly. He and Mother don't know any Mandarin. They hate the sound of the language and refuse to learn it. Aygul and I speak it in school, but never in front of them or our grandparents.

I build a fire and put the kettle on to boil. The light here is dim, and I stay close to the kitchen ledge, hoping they will pay no attention to me.

They speak only of the farm. The Chinese man asks if the water spigot in our yard has ever run dry, has Father rotated crops, what grows best? He waits impatiently for Father's answers to be translated. No one offers acknowledgment when I bring tea or seems to notice me standing quietly in the shadow.

It is when the cadre clears his throat, reaches into his black pouch, and lays papers on the eating cloth that my body goes numb.

"Teacher Cheng says that your daughter has excellent reports. That she is very educated." The smile on the cadre's face as he says this looks Chinese. He has forgotten he's Uyghur. He's a worse enemy than the Chinese. "She is the kind we are most proud to send away in our Surplus Work Force to help in the development of our great country," he adds, still smiling. He turns to the Chinese man and more or less repeats, in Mandarin, what he has just said.

The Chinese man folds his arms across his chest. He is not smiling.

Slowly, he lifts his head. As he pauses to form his words, Father breaks in, his eyes scary now, and black as coal.

"You pay my daughter the greatest honor," Father says in a cold, steely voice. "But you must be able to see that our family does not need the salary of a factory girl."

"No, no." The cadre waves his arms. He does not seem to have expected this interruption. "It is because of her extraordinary talents that she has been chosen. It will be our duty to see that she is given only the finest assignment." Suddenly his open palms go to his chest in a gesture of *salam* as if pleading with Father to understand that this is something he is being forced to do.

"What's going on?" The Chinese man's face is hard, with no expression. His narrowed eyes never blink as he listens to the cadre translate the words that have just been said.

Father steals a glance at me, and I nod. The translation is exact.

The silence that follows is more frightening than the words as the Chinese man glares at Father. Finally he raises an eyebrow.

"As the . . . incoming cadre of the district . . ." he says in halting Uyghur.

Father and I both flinch. There have been rumors that

the government is transferring Uyghur cadres away from their home districts so they won't show favoritism to relatives and friends, but I hadn't thought they might replace them with Chinese cadres.

"Perhaps," he is saying, in Mandarin now, "perhaps I can arrange for your daughter to stay here. If you are willing to give up your land. Sell it," he says, "for a sum we agree on." The dismissive gesture he makes with his hand cuts into me like a knife, and I wonder if I can keep upright as I listen to the translation and watch Father's face crumple.

But his eyes stay steely. He draws in short, quick breaths. I freeze, wait for him to erupt in anger. They'll arrest him. Send him away to a labor camp.

No, Father, I silently plead as I step from the shadow. *Don't!*

He does not see me.

When he speaks, his voice is deep and solemn.

"My family has farmed this land for generations," Father says. "It is a sacred trust to our ancestors that we continue to do so. If it's sold, where will we go? What will we do?" His voice has begun to falter. He looks over at me and hisses words through clenched teeth. "My daughter cannot be the price I must pay to keep our home."

The Chinese cadre—our new cadre—is smiling. He lets his arms fall to his sides as he listens to the translation of what has just been said, and for the first time seems comfortable sitting on the floor around our eating cloth.

I know then that I must go. What would Father do without the farm? And Grandfather—I can never be the one who forces my beloved grandfather from this land that was his father's, and his father's father's, and back and back beyond our knowing.

I walk on unsteady legs to the eating cloth and squat beside the men. "I will go," I say. "I have been chosen and I will fulfill my duty."

Father looks at me. Confused. Maybe angry that his daughter has spoken before these important men? I pretend I do not see his expression and pull the papers in front of him. I hand him the pen and point to where he must sign.

Then I rise and leave our house. I run past Mother, Aygul, Grandfather, Grandmother, across our fields and beyond the mulberry trees to the outermost boundary of our farm. In the distance, to the south, I see the Kunlun. Tall, majestic mountains, even in their shroud of dust and desert sand. These mountains sustain us, send us melted water from their ice caps, which flows freely into our rivers and underground streams. They make it possible for us to live beside the desert.

They are the edge of my world as I know it.

I will soon be sent beyond them.

Four

MY FEET NO LONGER connect to the earth. Some part of me has begun to seal off feeling. I don't want to think, I don't want to know. This is how I'll spend the next year. When I return, I'll erase from everyone's memory — first from my own — that I have been anyplace but here, walking across this field.

"Roshen, we must talk."

Father has surprised me.

I shake my head no. "It's done, Father," I say. I don't want to talk to him or see him right now.

His hand takes mine. "I have not signed the papers. I'm to give the cadre my answer tomorrow."

I close my eyes. I cannot face this good man. "They've chosen me. I will go," I say, but I feel my face beginning to contort into an ugly mask. "We will not lose this farm because of me." My words puncture the air as the anger I've been holding in for days spills out.

Father holds both of my hands now in a tight grip. "There may be another way. I'll speak to Uncle. A bribe may be enough to change the cadre's mind. Perhaps we can come up with enough money to satisfy him." His words are urgent, pleading, yet I know he only half believes them himself.

"He'll take the money *and* the farm. You know that. We've heard the stories." I'm calmer now. I draw in deep breaths and plant my feet in the precious soil of our land. "Father," I say, "our family has protected this land from the encroachment of the desert since time untold. We've been offered a chance to save it."

I take my hands from his tight grip and place them on his arms. "The teacher has spoken to me. I was especially chosen, she says, and will be given a wonderful opportunity to advance myself. She says it's important that Uyghur girls, especially those from the countryside, like me, have a broader view of the world, that it will enhance my opportunities for acceptance in the teacher training program and in finding a job." I sound like a prerecorded propaganda message, but my words seem to bring some comfort to Father.

"A year is a long time to be away from us," Father says.

"Yes," I say, and what strength I've found seeps from my body. I can't think what it will be like to be separated from them. Or from Ahmat.

Father sees me falter. His hand encircles my waist, and slowly he leads me to our waiting family.

Father will sign. I will go. And I have no idea what I will say to Ahmat, or what I want him to say to me.

Five

MOTHER AND I sit in silence around the eating cloth, drinking tea. Father hasn't returned, and Grandfather has long ago taken Grandmother and Aygul to the garden to weed the onions, then the melon patch.

The brakes from Uncle's truck squeal as he stops on the road. Mother rushes outside, but I stay where I am, squeezing my tea bowl almost to the breaking point. If I'm to learn that my life for the next year has been surrendered to the Chinese government, I wish to get the news sitting down.

Uncle's truck rumbles away. I hear two male voices crossing the yard—Father and another I know so well. I freeze as Ahmat follows Father through the door.

Our eyes lock.

I hear his silent cry. *Roshen!*

I twist my head away and bow in shyness—or is it because no muscles in my body work to hold my head upright? There is too much meaning in Father's return and Ahmat's arrival with him.

"We'll have tea and talk about my visit," Father says as the family gathers inside the house.

He and Ahmat sit across from me. Grandfather joins them.

Tea is poured. Mother, Grandmother, and Aygul sit. After we've raised our bowls for our first sip, Father begins.

"Your uncle and I were not able to buy your freedom, Roshen. You and eleven other Uyghur girls are to leave tomorrow morning." His voice falters to a whisper. "I'm sorry, my daughter."

My hands tremble as I nod in acceptance of Father's words.

We sit in silence until Grandfather takes another sip of tea. We do the same, rousing again to life.

"Thank you, Father, for bringing Ahmat to see me," I say.

"These are not normal times, Roshen. Our traditions are a path that may not always be followed," Father says. "Grandfather and I will go outside for a while so that you and Ahmat can talk freely. Your mother and grandmother will be your chaperones."

Mother asks Aygul to pour more tea for Ahmat and me. She clasps me close to her before rising and going to the kitchen ledge. Grandmother follows, and they busy themselves.

Ahmat comes to my side, squatting a respectful distance away. He's clutching his hands.

"What, Ahmat? . . . Tell me," I whisper.

"You must be careful." The urgency in his voice undoes his attempt to be quiet.

Aygul has heard him. Mother, too. She folds her arms around Aygul, moves her back to the ledge and the making of *naan*.

He leans toward me. "They wouldn't tell your father where they're taking you. No matter how awful it is, if they treat you badly, don't fight them, don't protest. Uyghurs never win. You'll end up in jail." His words come faster and faster. Then stop. The fear I'm feeling must show on my face. He straightens, closes his eyes for a moment.

"Roshen," he says, his hand creeping toward mine. Not quite meeting it. "Roshen, I'm here because they told your father you're not allowed to take, or use, phones or electronic devices. They believe it will make you homesick if you stay in contact with family. Your father thought I might know a way for us to communicate, and he's right. We'll set up a name and password." Ahmat is whispering now. "You'll need to find an internet café, one that operates in secret, with no connection to the government."

I hear his words. I want so much to take his hands and comfort him while he's here with me, and to have him comfort me.

But we should not touch, and we don't.

"Protect yourself," Ahmat says, and now his eyes bore even deeper into mine. "One of the girls could be a traitor, an informer, or a spy. Someone paid to report wrongdoing or disapproving comments about the government. Don't make friends until you're sure."

"I don't want to believe you, but I've heard that things can be bad." A shiver runs through my body. "Some girls never come back."

"I wish I could go in your place," Ahmat says with a tenderness that touches my heart. "But it's you they want. They hope you won't come back and marry me and bear our Uyghur children."

"No, Ahmat! We will marry. We'll have children. They can't rob us of that."

"You'll come back to me, Roshen. You're strong. Much stronger than you realize." Ahmat settles back on his heels. "I have something for you," he says. "I'd planned to give it to you after my mother spoke to your family about us. Please take it with you now—to remember me."

Ahmat reaches into his pocket and brings out a pendant of white jade that hangs from a delicate white ribbon. "I harvested this from the river this spring. It carries with it all the beauty of our Kunlun Mountains and the purity of the melting snow that carried it down the mountain to our river. Wear it, Roshen, with my promise of love and faithfulness to you while you're away." His voice catches, and he turns his face aside.

"Whatever happens, I will come back to you, Ahmat, as pure as this stone." Held-back tears choke my words.

I ask him to tie it on for me, then hold out my hand to

stop him. Aygul is watching. My eyes shoot daggers at her until she cocks her head, smiles, and scurries over to stand by Mother and Grandmother, who are still occupied at the kitchen ledge.

"It's all right now," I say quietly, and think only of the quiver in his hands as he places the jade piece on my chest, how his fingers linger as he smooths the ribbon around my neck, how they fumble to make the tie. Of the closeness of his body to mine as he kneels behind me.

I turn to him. "Thank you, Ahmat. Perhaps I'll find it easier to be away, having this token that binds us."

We are so close now that our lips almost touch. I think, I hope, that I might get the first kiss I've ever had. There can be nothing wrong with our lips meeting when we are pledged to each other and will be separated for so long.

There is noise outside. Father and Grandfather are returning.

In slow motion, Ahmat and I part, our lips never meeting.

We stand.

"Is it all right if Ahmat stays for a while, Father? I was just going to show him a poem I wrote."

"Of course," Father answers. "Our family will have time together this evening."

We sit again, my notebook now between us. We do not speak of my poem but make it appear that we do so.

Ahmat has me write out the string of letters and numbers to use when I send an email and read what he has sent to me. We plan code words with hidden meanings to make it safe for us to send good and bad news without alerting the internet police to dangerous words—like "Uyghur" or "Muslim" or "protest"—as our arms, like two magnets drawing together, touch. We pull apart, and now Ahmat's hand covers mine as I try to write one more code name. I should pull away, but I don't.

Our plan has to work. We can't be apart for a whole year with no word to each other.

And then it is time for him to leave.

Six

I HAVE BEEN ORDERED to go to the bus yards on the outer edge of Hotan. It's a long distance for our donkey, so Uncle drives us in his truck. A few girls already stand beside a rundown plum-colored van that has been driven far too many times across the desert and over unpaved mountain roads. A Chinese woman with broad shoulders and a large face that seems all mouth and teeth holds a clipboard. Father has been assured I will be safe and well cared for under the protection of a guardian — and I know instantly it will be more important to be protected *from* her. Nothing hides the meanness in her eyes.

I don't express my fear to Father. We exchange a quick farewell; our goodbyes took place last night.

I pause a moment to study the girls before I approach the matron. Some are chatting together. I think these are city girls from Hotan, the way they're dressed. They wear no headscarves, their skirts are short, and they don't wear leggings. They could be Chinese except for their Uyghur faces and the soft gracefulness of their movements. Other girls stand apart, each with a suitcase or satchel beside her, the small collection of belongings each of us is allowed to bring.

"I am Roshen," I tell the matron in Mandarin.

She looks at her clipboard. A slash of her pencil suggests I've been marked off. She lifts her face and grins at me. "My name is Ushi," she says, and I hear a snicker coming from one of the girls.

The matron bristles. Her fists tighten. She does not turn in the direction of the insult, but I'm certain that if there were not parents present, she would happily slap the offender in the face.

Another newcomer distracts the matron as I back away and go to stand with the girls who wear headscarves. I assume we all speak some Mandarin, but I think I know which girl had the courage to snicker—the girl who knew that *Ushi* means "ox" in Mandarin. Her eyes are pinched into narrow slits, her eyebrows drawn together as if protecting herself from the glare of the sun. But the sun today is masked in a haze of sand and dust from the desert. The anger I feel in my heart shows on her face. I think we'll be friends.

When all the parents have left, we're told to throw our bags on the roof, where they're lashed down with ropes. Ushi herds us into the van. "Five of you have to fit into the back. *Yee, er,*" she counts as she half lifts two girls from the ground and shoves them through the door. "You two skinny ones, go to the back with them," she says. "And you. Why are you here, Mouse?" She's shaking her head as she pulls at a young girl, maybe fourteen, tiny, her face almost completely shrouded in a black and white striped scarf. I wonder what family has had to sell their daughter to the Surplus Work Force so they might have enough to eat.

The rest of us scarf people are sent to the middle row of seats, four of us in a seat meant for three. I'm the first in, followed by the angry one, then a quiet one with beautiful long black hair that falls below her scarf. The last one holds back when she sees little room for her to sit. "You there, girl," Ushi says, bearing down on her and grabbing her sleeve. "Get in."

"My name is Adile," the girl says as she pulls her arm away and steps into the van. And it doesn't matter that we're crushed together. We do not know one another, yet we somehow become one. I'm sure our bond will help us endure a matron who clearly finds it beneath her to deal with Uyghurs.

Our linked bodies seem to share a moment of amusement rather than jealousy when we watch the great swishing of long hair and oversize earrings as the three unscarved girls climb into the rusty old plum-colored van as if going on holiday. They take the seats in the front row. Three seats for three girls. Their short skirts and uncovered hair have apparently brought them privilege. I don't think any of these girls is an informer. Wouldn't that person be squashed in among us, wearing a headscarf and clothing that covers more of her body?

Ushi closes the door and climbs into her seat beside the driver.

No one speaks as the van leaves the bus yard and heads

onto the road. We are out beyond the open market, but we pass donkey carts bringing in goods to sell. Families. A mother, a father, a baby swaddled in spite of the heat; an old grandfather, alone, driving his donkey. I see in every one of them the vision of my family, and I want to reach out and stop them. No. I want them to stop me from hurtling down this road to places where I've never been.

That's not to be, and I see the memory of all I know in the poplars that line our way. *Go quickly, please,* I silently plead to our driver. Let our destination be only a big, ugly factory with no memories attached to it, only Ushi and her comrades barking orders. I don't want to see anything that will remind me of the people and places I know.

A motorcycle passes the van—it could be Ahmat. Now I can't breathe. I'm next to an open window. I lean out. Can I jump? It's Ahmat, and he's borrowed a motorcycle and come to rescue me. We'll ride off into a forbidden unknown, escape across a border, and if we live through that, maybe find happiness somewhere in this world.

But it isn't Ahmat on the motorcycle.

I ease back into my seat and close my eyes. My hands fold over my jade pendant, which lies hidden under my blouse. It's the same blouse I wore yesterday, and I'm certain the scent of him lingers on it—and he is here with me. He's tying a ribbon around my neck. Our lips almost . . . almost touch in a kiss. That memory I will always keep with me, concealed in my heart where it cannot be reached. Ushi can command my presence, but not my being.

When I open my eyes again, the road is a straight, paved pathway through the desert. Flowing sand dunes line our way in ever-changing patterns. I might find some comfort in the strange beauty of this landscape if not for the oil tankers thundering past us and the unwelcome jabber from the girls in the front seats—harsh, sharp sounds of Mandarin. I guess they're trying to impress Ushi with their proficiency, their eagerness to begin a new life.

The four of us in my row do not seem to have moved at all—then I see that isn't true. The girl with the long black hair bends over a square of cotton, silently moving a needle in and out of her embroidery.

I stretch and try to shift. I've grown numb. Now everyone moves a fraction.

"We'll be packed in like this for the next two or three days, before we even get to the train." It's the girl next to me who speaks. The angry one.

I nod, but I have no words. No one does. Until we hear a soft voice from behind us. "I have to go to the toilet." It's the mouse.

"Hey, Ushi," the angry one calls out in Mandarin. "We have to stop in the next town. We have to pee."

Ushi turns around, and all we see are teeth and grin. "There's a public WC two hours up ahead. We'll probably stop there," she says.

I feel every muscle in my seatmate's body tense, but she remains silent. Then she twists around. "I'm afraid you're going to have to wait. Can you do that?" the angry one asks in Uyghur, her voice now gentle and caring. It surprises me.

"I'll try," the girl answers in a whisper. Her hand covers her eyes, that little part of her face that is visible underneath her black and white striped scarf.

"What's your name?" my seatmate asks. "You must never let anyone call you Mouse."

"Zuwida."

"That's a beautiful name. My name is Mikray."

I half stand so I can reach across the back of the seat to touch the young girl's arm, to try to offer some comfort. "Hello, Zuwida. My name is Roshen."

"My name is Gulnar," says the embroiderer.

"You already know that my name is Adile," our fourth seatmate says.

"I'm Jemile," says one of the waifs in the back seat, the one with the sweetest, most innocent face. Another who cannot possibly be more than fourteen years old.

The remaining three introduce themselves: Patime and Letipe, who are sisters, they say, and Nurbiya. Now nine of us—the scarf girls—have names. For a moment I forget about watching for traitors as we chat quietly about sand dunes, the plantings at the sides of the road that help to reduce erosion, the sandstorm that seems to be brewing off to the northeast, way out across the desert plain. We wonder if it will sweep to the south. If we will drive into it. If it might delay us. No one speaks of home, of food or water, or of having to pee.

Then we stop speaking, comforted perhaps by the awareness that we're not totally alone, that we have shared some little part of ourselves. The motion of the van, the rhythm of the tires turning on the asphalt, lulls us as we speed across the desert and through small towns.

Perhaps I fall asleep or drift into some unconscious state, but I pull back to reality when Ushi shrieks. The van is careening across the highway toward a massive wall of flying steel. I'll be killed! Incinerated when we hit—with everyone else who's been thrown against me. Pushing me to my death.

We miss the end of the tanker by a few grains of sand and now face head-on the stream of approaching trucks and tankers, horns blasting as they try to dodge us. Our driver keeps jerking the wheel as we thump along against traffic. I scream, waiting for the collision that will send our body parts across the desert.

But we're alive. We made it! To the sand along the wrong side of the road. We sit in the van, stunned, with arms, legs, bodies sprawled all over one another. Ushi erupts into a string of swear words at the driver, who sits ashen behind the wheel.

"He couldn't help it," Adile says to us quietly. "It's a blowout. I know. My family has a truck."

"Everyone out!" Ushi shouts. We push and stumble through the door until our feet touch solid ground and we take in deep breaths of hot desert air.

Slowly, we seem to regain awareness that we really

have survived, and again form into our scarf and no-scarf groups. Except for Zuwida, who cowers beside the van. This may be our chance to help, if she hasn't already wet her pants. With Mikray's assistance, I get the scarf girls to enclose Zuwida in a tight ring to shield her from the passing trucks and cars so she can squat and relieve herself with as little humiliation as possible. The three scarfless ones notice and come toward us. This is sure to alert Ushi, who could well inflict more embarrassment upon Zuwida for her uncontrollable bladder. I leave the circle and go toward the scarfless girls.

"What are you doing?" the girl who seems to be the leader of the three asks, and I wonder why she suddenly cares. Maybe she too has to pee.

"We're helping someone," I say in Uyghur. "Please don't draw attention to us. Could you talk to Ushi? Distract her, so she doesn't notice?"

I'm met with a collective shrug, but the girl who asked looks over at the group again before turning away. I follow her, tap her on the shoulder. "We'll help you, too, if you need it." For a moment our eyes meet. Then with a jerk of her head she walks away, heading for our matron, who is frantically looking at her watch and at the driver, who is struggling with the tire. And then I can't see Ushi because the girl and her followers line up to block her vision.

There is little talk as we file back into the van and wait to move across oncoming traffic to our lane. Soon we are heading again toward the unknown. Gulnar takes out her embroidery. Perhaps some do as I do—listen to the scarfless trio chat in Mandarin about French fashion and glossy lipstick. Their leader, I learn, is Hawa. Rayida sits next to her, tilting her head this way and that, always smiling, looking for approval. The third girl remains nameless. She's dressed like the other two in a little short skirt and formfitting blouse. It's amusing to see her try to mimic their gestures, try to be part of their conversation when they ignore her. It's sad, too.

Will I ever wish to be other than I am? Other than the girl who wears Ahmat's necklace?

We all become alert as we approach an oasis and the dunes give way to grass and trees. We drive into a town where shops spill out onto the sidewalk and people who look like us are buying tomatoes and peppers or sitting under umbrellas scooping *polo* into their mouths.

Mikray shoves against me, and we both lean out the window and shout *"Salam!"* to everyone who is Uyghur. We pass donkey carts, old men in big black woolly hats, women in all kinds of colorful headscarves. Soon everyone is leaning out the windows calling—until Ushi hollers *"Zhu zui!"* We sink back into our seats and shut up as commanded. I don't know why we obey. Maybe we're all afraid she won't let us use a toilet and we'll have to soil our clothes.

A blare of Chinese music comes from a huge loudspeaker suspended on a pole, high above the street where we have stopped for a traffic signal. Before we pass, the music changes to a voice telling us we must work hard to make China a great nation. I wonder if someone knows we're here and is talking just to us. The voice makes me shiver.

The whole town makes me shiver. Just as in Hotan, piles of mud bricks that were once Uyghur homes lie beside new buildings for the Han Chinese, who apparently need big, ugly places to live in and want us to be the same. Cranes loom beside half-built office buildings that reach high into the sky.

The van pulls over to the side of the road. There is a plaza in front of one of the fancier buildings, and there beside two struggling, spindly trees is the public WC. We're allowed to go in two at a time, starting, of course, with the first row. When it comes to Gulnar and Mikray's turn, Ushi tells Mikray to stay in her seat. I crawl over her and Adile and go in with Gulnar. Then two from the back seat go in, and two more, which leaves Zuwida sitting there.

"You'll go in with me, Mouse," Ushi says. "The driver is in charge of you others while I'm inside." She looks directly at Mikray as she says this.

Mikray sits as still as stone. I want to say something, but I don't know if our driver understands Uyghur or not, so I do not speak.

Ushi returns and calls for Mikray. "You'll go by yourself," she says. "I'll have none of your troublemaking." She walks Mikray to the WC and sends her in—alone. I say a silent prayer. Ushi could have torn Mikray limb from limb if she'd chosen to, and none of us would have known what happened. I fear that Mikray carries a knife, as a Uyghur man would, and I'm sure she knows how to use it.

As we pull out again into the busy roadway, Ushi reaches into a box on the floor of the van and hands back twelve bottles of water. It seems an act of kindness—we're all thirsty from the heat—until I think that she's probably being paid to deliver us alive and we do at least require water. Each row is then handed one small bag of salted dried peas and one small bag of spicy peanuts to share. The amount we are to eat is apparently determined by our status in Ushi's eyes.

The taste of a few peas and nuts leaves a gnawing hunger in my stomach. For food. For home. For my life as it was. I reach into the purse that hangs from my shoulder, the purse that holds the yuan Father gave me, the only money I'll have until I earn my own. It holds a packet of raisins, emergency food Mother insisted I take along—and the emergency is now. The grapes were raised on our farm, harvested by my sister and me, sun-dried on our roof. It's not my hunger I feed, it is the longing for what I've left behind.

Even as I savor the taste, I know I will share. With a touch on Mikray's arm I pass the bag along. She takes a few raisins and passes it on until there is a tap on my shoulder and the empty bag is returned to me from the back row. In this way some dried fruit appears, a few nuts from deep inside someone's pocket.

We scarf girls feast on a small taste of home.

Seven

THE SANDSTORM WE WATCHED rise in a giant swirl over the desert now covers us, creating darkness as we creep along the highway through a blanket of sand. The scarfless trio keeps us informed of the hour and our destination with their endless questions to Ushi, who answers with surprising politeness—perhaps her boss will reward her for delivering these princesses of beauty and high fashion to him. It's rumored that bosses like pretty girls. Our modesty will be our protection.

It is evening when we arrive in Cherchen. Silhouettes of trees now line our way. Traffic lights blink hazy warnings that our driver ignores because no one else seems to be driving through the streets. We finally stop and are herded into a hotel. Ushi picks up keys and escorts us to the second floor, where she opens two doors. "Okay," she says, "six in each room. There's a bed and chairs you can sleep on. The toilet's in the hall. Dinner downstairs in ten minutes." Which would be useful information if any one of us had a watch.

"Will our bags be brought to us?" Hawa asks.

"No one is going back out into that storm to get your bags, honey," Ushi answers in a horrible, mocking voice as she opens the door to another room and disappears.

We'll spend the night in our clothes, which are damp, sweaty rags. We have all endured the sweltering heat inside the closed-up van. Even a slit of open window would have buried us in sand. What was I thinking when I chose to wear my most precious blouse for this journey—the filmy, soft, reddish-orange blouse I had on when I said goodbye to Ahmat? I rush into a room—either room, it doesn't matter—and curl up in a chair. I'll stay here all night while my blouse collects more sweat, and tears if I have any left in me.

The gentle touch on my arm is Zuwida's. Mikray is standing behind her. "We want you to come to dinner with us," Zuwida says, and I do.

We're divided between two round tables. Each has a wooden circle in the middle that holds plates of food. It can be spun around so that the dish you want is right in front of you. We ooh and aah at the abundance of the food, at this sudden generosity—until an unfamiliar smell fills our nostrils and we lean back. We're being served Chinese food—pork food—and we will not eat it. Even the rice smells so strong we know it's tainted with pork broth.

Ushi has to know that Muslims don't eat pork. Uyghur families do not eat pork even if they're not religious. I look over at the next table, where Hawa sits. Her plate is full of food; a pair of the chopsticks they've given to each of us is in her hand, but she does not use them. I watch as she lays them down at the side of her plate. Not one of the twelve girls is eating. If one is a traitor, she, too, is going hungry.

A waitress leaves a pot of tea at our table. We take turns pouring it into the small bowls at our places. We drink. That is our supper.

Ushi and the driver eat much of what is at their table, then come to ours and remove the dishes of their favorite foods. They chat as if nothing strange is happening. When they're done eating, we are escorted to our rooms. It is fortunate the toilet is in the hallway, or we might have been locked in.

———

Mikray wakes me. I open my eyes enough to know that it's dark and I'm curled up in a chair with my clothes on. "Come with me. Bring yuan," she whispers. And I, who have lived carefully all my life, follow her into the hallway and out onto the street—not knowing why and not caring.

The storm has subsided, with only bits of sand and grit lingering in the air. Streaks of dawn break through the nighttime skies, lighting our way as we cross the wide highway in front of our hotel and head into a maze of windy, unpaved streets. Our cheap hotel is next to the Uyghur part of town. Mikray must have been paying attention enough last night to know this.

I've guessed our mission. "I smell naan," I say. We turn down an alley and find a woman loading flatbread onto a cart. We bargain for six loaves. Without saying so, we seem to have agreed we'll share with everyone—half a loaf each can be hidden and will sustain us for a while.

It's taken more time than we hoped. The sun has risen and so has Ushi. She's talking to the manager as we slip inside. We've at least been wise enough to cover the naan with our skirts, but it's obvious we're hiding something. The manager has seen us and must have told Ushi, because Ushi turns around just as we start up the stairs. "You, girl, what are you doing down here?"

Girl? And she's right. Mikray has disappeared. I'm the one caught, and Ushi heads toward me. I bow my head, bring my free hand to my heart. "I'm sorry. . . . I'm sorry," I keep saying over and over in Mandarin until an excuse comes. "I'd . . . I had hoped to find the van. It's that time of the month," I whisper. I hope my face gets red, although it's absurd to think I might have found the van, untied the luggage, heaved it around, and found my bag. "I need something—desperately. I should have asked you first. I know. I'm sorry." I look at her now and try to make my eyes innocent. "Please let me go back to my room. Maybe one of the girls can help me."

Ushi heads toward me. My hand shakes, and I can feel the loaves slipping from my grip. I press against the wall. *Please don't let me drop them.* But I'm going to. I grab the bottom of the loaves with my other hand, clutching them through my skirt. *I'm too hungry to let Ushi steal my naan!* I work the round flatbreads to the center of my belly, gather more of my skirt, and bunch it between my legs, two hands now grabbing my crotch. "I must get to a toilet," I say, and I flee up the stairs and run down the hallway to the WC. It's empty, or so I think until I see the legs of someone in the stall. "Mikray?" I whisper. "How did you get here?"

"What did the fat ox do to you?" she says, and steps out.

"You left me alone!" Fear and anger mix as I lash out. I hate that she chose me to go with her. And that I went.

Mikray's face falls for a second before the hard line of her eyebrows re-forms. "I'm sorry," she says as she fastens me with a cold look. "I mistook you for someone who'd want to help. I won't do it again." She turns to march out the door at the same time Ushi bursts through.

Ushi stops. Her gaze shifts from Mikray to me. "You chose this one to help you?" She points to Mikray. "Be careful," she says. "I don't think you want to get involved with her kind." Glaring at Mikray, Ushi seems to have forgotten my transgression.

"Breakfast downstairs. Now. Tell the others," she says, and heads out the door.

For an awkward second nothing is said.

"Take your naan to the unscarved ones. I won't go near that room," Mikray says, and leaves.

———

The steamed pork buns they serve for breakfast are eaten by Ushi and our driver. As we're ushered through the lobby to the van, Mikray comes up beside me. "There's another stairway down the hall." I follow her glance, and there it is, in plain sight. "I had to leave you. We'd never have saved the naan if I'd been caught with you. Ushi would have suspected the worst.

"You're sweet enough to get away with anything," Mikray says as she moves away.

Sweet? All I feel is hate. Hate for Mikray, who got me into trouble and is now squashed against me in the van. I turn away, and I'm looking across the street at the Uyghur neighborhood. Why didn't I see it the night before? Why didn't I know there was a back stairway and sneak away, leaving Mikray standing alone? What was her life like before to make her so sly?

Somehow I know at this very moment that I'll never again be the person I was when I left home. I'm traveling beyond the mountains, and I have much to learn. I'm glad Mikray chose me. I'm proud that I helped to fill our bellies for a few hours. Being "sweet" is a defense I'll gladly use.

"There are some rules you apparently don't understand," Ushi says, turning in her seat to face us as we drive off through yellow, dust-filled air. "Let's get it straight. You don't wander off by yourself. You ask me if you need help." Her words are slow and snarly. Her eyes dart around the van until she finds me. "Do we *all* understand that now?" Her eyes don't leave me, and I will not bow my head or look away. For awful moments she holds her stare and I hold mine. "I understand," I say in a meek, quiet voice.

I give her what she wants so I can break her rule again. *Be sweet,* I tell myself.

Ushi rewards me with a grin and teeth and turns away.

Eight

WE'RE IN A HURRY to get somewhere. Ushi looks at her watch. Prods the driver. I'm waiting for the next blowout, wondering how a road can go on and on so endlessly through this barren land.

Hours pass. We come to a rather large city. When it's obvious we're not going to stop, I break off a small piece of the naan hidden in my bag. I cover my mouth as I chew, even though I'm sure Ushi is too busy cursing traffic lights and slow drivers to be looking at me in the rearview mirror. Even the princesses in the front seats are careful to turn away when they sneak bits of naan from their bags or pockets. No sign yet that a traitor has reported Mikray's and my wrongdoing. Perhaps hunger triumphs over treachery.

There's little talk in the van until we start bouncing around, the road now ridged and uneven, as the driver speeds along, not caring if we're jostled from our seats. We laugh—giggly, silly laughs—although it isn't at all funny. Then someone says that maybe the mountains up ahead are our own Kunlun and maybe our mountains won't let us pass through.

"'I am far from my homeland and the sky is gray.'" I

say softly to myself the words that well in my heart, words taught to me by my father. "'The moon is good, the sun is good, to be a wanderer is bad.'" A small voice joins me from the seat in back, and I know it is Zuwida. It surprises me that she is the one who knows our poetry. "'I am a wanderer, the prince of wanderers. I cannot bear this wandering, my face is sallow,'" we finish together. Everyone listens. An unnatural stillness settles over us.

Ushi turns. Stares. She cannot know the meaning of our Uyghur Muqam, our songs and poems, but it's obvious she didn't like the private moment that just passed among us.

"Oh," Hawa says, her voice high and little-girlish as she leans toward Ushi. "It's all so *different* here. Where are we? We . . . were wondering."

That is not what we were doing, but it's a good fake. The road winds along a narrow river canyon, and walls of solid rock engulf us.

Ushi looks at Hawa and rolls her eyes. "Yeah, it's different," she says. "If we can get there, we're going to climb the mountain up ahead and go down the other side." She rolls her eyes again, shrugs, and turns to face the front.

She's right to wonder "if we can get there." The road is nothing like our sandy, poplar-lined roads back home— slow, reliable, and just fine for ambling donkey carts. Here the van struggles along a track of dirt and stones. We come to a stream, and the driver plunges in and by some miracle gets us to the other side. The road keeps winding and we keep crisscrossing the riverbed. Ushi is no longer paying any attention to us. She spews out more curse words than I've ever heard.

Then the road climbs the mountain. We zigzag back and forth, up and up. Too often, the window on my side looks out over the huge emptiness that lies below—the void we'll plunge into if our van has another blowout—and my stomach feels hollow.

I clutch the white jade in my hands. Need its comfort. Need Ahmat to keep me safe. Wait to be overcome by loneliness so I can't think about plunging over the cliff. It doesn't work. My breath is short. I push against the back of the seat, afraid to move. Afraid to open my eyes. "Are you all right?" Mikray asks, and I can't answer. I want to crawl on the floor, to cling to something safe, and all I have to cling to is my necklace.

I squeeze my eyes more tightly shut and make a foolish plea to Ahmat to rescue me as we keep going up the narrow switchbacks that climb the embankments. What is it I fear most? Falling from this great height—or being on the other side of the mountain?

We stop. I force my eyes open. This spot seems safe. We've cut through a pass, and there is a low rock outcropping on the abyss side of the road to keep us from plunging over.

"Everyone out. Stretch. Do whatever you have to. You may have noticed there are no towns or WCs along this route," Ushi says.

We pile out. The thought of seeing Ushi squatting and peeing on the side of the road helps me forget that my legs feel shaky and my breath comes in shallow pants. My head swims when I look out into space. I go quickly to the mound of rocks—lean into it.

There's commotion near the van. "What is it now, Mouse? You're a needy little thing, aren't you?" Ushi says as she bears down on Zuwida.

I see Mikray holding back, shooting looks of hate at Ushi. Adile is with Zuwida, and I must be there too. *Focus,* I tell myself. *Look only at Zuwida.* And I do it; I walk to her. The drop into the abyss is on the other side of the van.

Zuwida rubs her forehead; her nose is bleeding. "Got a little headache, right? Nosebleed?" Ushi says, shoving some tissues at her. "It happens. We're up about four thousand meters. You'll be okay when we come down.

"Do whatever you have to, everyone. Let's get on our way." Ushi walks to the other side of the van. She'll probably squat there. I have no desire to watch her. I want only to push her off the cliff.

We've encountered just one vehicle on this road so far, a truck carrying a load of sheep in the other direction, so we don't fear being seen. Even so, we form our protective circle and take turns relieving ourselves, two at a time.

We're all shivering. It's colder up here, but I don't care. The clean, pure smell of the air refreshes my mind—perhaps too much. As I massage my arms to keep warm, the soft feel of my blouse stirs memories I can't allow myself to have. We're herded back into the van, and I think of keeping my eyes focused on the ground, and of the new seat arrangements. Adile will sit in back with Zuwida, and I will be in the middle of my row, away from the windows.

I sit next to Gulnar, and her embroidery helps me over the mountain. She brings the cloth from her pocket. The needle is threaded with pink floss, and I see she is adding flowers to the brown stems and green leaves she has already sewn, flowers that grow along the long spikes at the branch tips. Her needle moves in and out of the cloth; now she wraps thread around the needle and adds the coils in some magical way so that it looks as if the flower petal is real, not flat but growing upward, out from the stem. She pulls another thread from her pocket, bites off the length she needs, rethreads her needle, and keeps working. The floss is deeper pink in color this time. I watch as a full, four-petaled, rose-pink flower rises from the stem. Gulnar is creating a tamarisk bush, one of the few plants that can survive in the desert, on her cloth.

I watch her with every fiber of my body, and even so, I know when we come too close to the edge. Gulnar's fingers tighten; her needle moves more slowly. The chatter—Uyghur behind me, Mandarin in front—has a slower pace, as if everyone is holding back breath.

We make it safely down the mountain. Ushi rewards us with water and more snacks of dried peas and spicy nuts as we drive through bleak and rocky mountain valleys. We pass a lake; a pack of camels nearby munch on something that must sustain them. Then, up ahead, I see a land of white —the air, the ground, everything is white, and it's not snow.

Chalky white dust is blowing in and settling on us. "Close your windows," Ushi says, and we obey. She pulls a mask from her bag to cover her nose and mouth, so it must really be bad. She hands a mask to the driver but offers none to us. Apparently Uyghurs do not require protection.

"What is happening?" Hawa asks.

"Mining. Grinding up rock."

We can see that. A ghostly white factory looms in the distance; huge machines crawl around in the white cloud, shoveling mounds of something white into small hills; trucks carry away large white bags in both directions, over the mountain and to wherever the road ahead leads. We drive into a tiny town and I see a sign: SHIMIANKUANG. It takes me a while, but I figure it out. *Kuang* means mine; *shi mian* could mean asbestos. We're driving through an asbestos mine. The Chinese don't even try to hide it!

We already have asbestos dust covering us, and more seeps in through the windows, even though they're closed. It might not kill us, but I know that breathing it in is bad. I rip a small piece of paper from the notebook I carry, write *asbestos* on it, and hand it to Gulnar, who quickly passes it on to the others. I untie my scarf and wrap it over my nose and mouth.

The note comes back to me and I pass it forward. If they haven't guessed, the three unscarved girls now know they're breathing asbestos. They, like the rest of us, are probably aware of what that means. Several men from Hotan were sent to work in the mines and returned with lung disease; two of them died. Word spread throughout our townships.

Mercifully, after a few kilometers we drive out of the mine to a paved road taking us through a mostly barren, flat valley. No one comments on the landscape anymore; oil derricks are of little interest. But when a town of some size appears, the hope that we might actually stop and get out of the van rouses us.

"Is this where we spend the night?" Mikray speaks loudly enough so she's sure Ushi hears her over honking horns and noisy motorcycles. The sun, the shadows tell us it's nearly nightfall—we've been traveling since early morning.

Ushi's laugh is repulsive. I have never had to know such loathing as I feel for this woman right now.

"Don't you wish," Ushi says. "We'll stop for the stinking toilet in the bus station. A few hours after that, you'll be on a train. That's lots of fun too." She looks directly at Mikray—a hard, cold look. Mikray is not wise; she should keep quiet. Ushi won't forget.

A filthy pit toilet. Then we're each handed a container of chicken-flavored instant noodles. In the middle of the night our luggage is thrown down to us and we're escorted from the van into the hard-seat car of train number T266. We don't know where we're going. Ushi has our tickets.

Nine

STEPPING INTO THE TRAIN is exciting. I've never ridden on a train. That seems true for many of us. We eagerly crowd aboard with the other passengers, only to find the seats already full and people standing in the aisles. Ushi sweeps by us, a man in uniform in tow. They yank people from their seats and push us into them.

"Why are you doing that? They were here first," Mikray says, pushing past everyone to get to Ushi.

"We paid for these seats. They paid for standing room. Now sit down and shut up," Ushi says, shoving Mikray into the empty seat next to the one where she's already put me.

"I'm sorry," Mikray says to the Chinese woman whose seat she has taken.

"It's all right," the woman says, smiling at Mikray. "I've been enjoying your seat for many hours. It's your turn."

Again, I wonder about myself. Who am I? Who is Mikray? Why didn't I say something to the woman whose seat I took? It would be awful to have to stand or squat in the aisle of a train because you can't afford a regular ticket. I'm grateful to have a seat, even though it's hard, with a high, straight back. Barely padded. I need sleep.

I find odd amusement in the thought that Ushi could have bought us standing room and just one hard seat for herself. I see her giving money to the man in uniform. I nudge Mikray and point behind us to make sure she sees it too. Then Ushi makes her way down the aisle. "It's a long trip," she says. "Don't leave these seats. I'll know if you do. You're being watched."

Admonishments delivered, Ushi disappears through the door at the end of our car.

"Great! The conductor spies on us while Ushi spends the night in the sleeper car." Mikray spits the words out. "Why'd she bother to pay him? None of us has enough money to get off the train and disappear—unless that one does." She points to Hawa, sitting across the aisle from us with the other two. They're on the three-seats-for-three-people side of the car. Mikray and I are on the other side, the two-seats-for-two-people side. I'm by the window, so Mikray and Hawa are separated only by the two Chinese women standing in the aisle.

"Why do you dislike Hawa? Do you know her?" The train is noisy. I can ask questions without anyone overhearing.

"Her name is Hawargul. I used to go to school with her. I don't know why she's here. Her father could have paid the fine to keep her off the list. She seemed to have everything she wanted." Mikray shrugs, lowers her head. I know there's more to tell.

"What else?" I ask.

"She and her friends hung out at the daytime disco clubs, dressed in their little short skirts, trying to look French or American. They didn't want to be Chinese, but they tried hard not to be Uyghur. I, on the other hand, made certain everyone knew I was Uyghur and I was proud of it. We had a standoff. . . . It's complicated," Mikray says as I watch her lips tighten, her cheekbones rise up almost to her narrowed eyes. Her face is striking. Strong beneath the orange and blue flowered scarf that she wears drawn tightly across her forehead.

"You are strong and powerful, Mikray. And fierce. You're a hard person to like, but I like you. I admire you."

She bites her lips. Her face softens. Her eyes cloud quickly with tears.

"Thank you," she whispers. She closes her eyes and turns away.

I call upon a cherished remembrance as I try to go to sleep. I'm stretched out on my sleeping platform with my sister, Aygul, at my side, Mother and Father close by. It's a safe, quiet place that doesn't stink of unwashed passengers, rotting food, and a smelly toilet. In reality I squeeze myself into a tight ball, my knees under my chin, my arms wrapped around my legs. Mikray does the same, and we lean back to back for support. I drift into a fitful sleep until the unforgiving stiffness of the seat leaves me numb and I have to shift position — or is it a voice that wakes me? Adile is shaking me. Shaking Mikray. She and Zuwida are sitting behind us, and Zuwida is sick. Nauseous. Headache. She does not feel better after coming down from the mountain as Ushi said she would. She feels worse.

By now the Chinese women sitting on their luggage in the aisle show concern. I explain in Mandarin what's happening. They know about mountain sickness. One woman touches her forehead to Zuwida's, takes her pulse. She gives Zuwida a pill. We have no comfort to offer; we have to trust that their remedy is sensible.

"That will help her headache. I'll fix a tea that will bring sleep," the woman says. "She's a frail child, isn't she?"

I really see Zuwida for the first time. The scarf she wears as a kind of shroud around her head and shoulders has been loosened, revealing the thinness of her little round face, the fragility of her neck and shoulders. I think she must have a sad story to tell of why she's here.

———

Night becomes day, and still we speed through a mostly barren landscape. A few yak herders watch over large, shaggy-haired oxen, which roam with their heads down, foraging for food. It's the reverse inside the train. Ushi, the ox-named one, brings us something to eat—another container of chicken-flavored noodles and water—then leaves for the comfort of her sleeper car.

Midmorning, things begin to change. The Chinese women tell us we're coming into the city of Xining, where they will be getting off the train. They are worried about

Zuwida. They leave us with two kinds of tea that we are to keep giving her, one for the sickness, the other to help her sleep; they leave a thermos, which is still half-filled with hot water. Even though we are now in a valley with mountains around us, we are quite high up, they say, on the outermost edge of the Tibetan plateau. She will need the medicine in the teas.

Saying goodbye is difficult. Their gentleness and kindness have sustained us through the night. We don't care that they are Chinese, that they don't know our language.

It is painful to see the longing in Zuwida's eyes as they embrace her and bid her a safe journey.

Ten

TWENTY-TWO AND A HALF hours after leaving Xining, we arrive in Wuhan. I have long since lost sense of day or night, but even as we trudge behind Ushi, making our way through crowds of people and a sickly gray smog, I know it's morning.

"You'll wait here," Ushi says, ushering us into a hall with rows and rows of hard gray seats, not unlike the ones we just left. None of the seats are empty, but we don't need more sitting. Our eyes follow Ushi until she is swallowed up in the crowds. Then we look at one another.

"Wuhan is the capital of Hubei Province." I say this in Mandarin, mimicking a teacher. "It is the most populous city in central China. It has a population of over ten million people." By now Mikray, Adile, and the others have joined in. We've all been forced to memorize these words and recite them in civics classes since we were young children.

We laugh, not because it is funny. I think we can't believe we're really here, alone in this huge city so distant from life in our desert oasis. Maybe we laugh because we're dirty and sweaty and tired and hungry, and to stand here and scream would take too much energy.

Ushi returns. We struggle to follow her, pushing and shoving like everyone else to make our way through the huge crowds until we come to the back of the station. We're marched to a delivery truck with the words HUBEI WORK WEAR CO. painted on the side. The van is not new and shiny, but the lettering is bright blue and unscratched. The driver approaches us. He bows his head. He smiles. "Welcome," he says in a language that is not quite Mandarin, and I remember that many here speak a Sichuan dialect. "Welcome to the Hubei Work Wear Company," he says, and bows again. I am pleased that I can understand him and start to acknowledge his welcome, but he is going to the back of the truck and opening the doors, gesturing for us to enter. We are to be delivered to our factory like common work wear.

There are no seats, but the floor where we are to squat is relatively clean. He closes the doors, sealing us into the stifling hot, airless cargo box. A bit of light filters in through the two small windows in the back doors. We're thrown off balance as the truck picks up speed and careens into the horn-honking, jam-packed roadway that leads to and from the station.

Mikray gets up, lurches to the doors. "We should have disappeared in the train station," she says. "There are places to hide in a city with ten million people." She swipes her hands over the doors. "There are no handles. We've been locked in like prisoners. It's pretty clear we're not being taken to a classy factory. We're going to be slaves, forced to do jobs nobody else wants." She turns, glares at us. "They can't do this. Treat us like animals. We have to—"

Zuwida starts coughing, a dry, hacking cough she can't stop, and Mikray ends her outburst. We turn our attention to Zuwida. We've come down from the high altitudes —why isn't she better? I crawl over to her. Adile holds her hand and I rub her back with gentle strokes. "We've run out of hot water," I say. "Maybe we can get some for you soon."

"What good will that do?" Mikray kneels in front of Zuwida too. "We've run out of the teas. Where will we get more?" She tries to restrain her voice, but Zuwida has heard. She reaches her hand out to Mikray.

"It's all right," she says. "I often cough, but it stops. I'm feeling better, really I am. I'm just tired." She tries to smile, but her lips are quivering. "I'll be glad when we get there," she whispers, her voice full of tears.

Adile puts her arm around Zuwida and draws her nearer until her head rests on Adile's shoulder. I gently lay my fingers on Zuwida's forehead to soothe her, to let her know it is safe to close her eyes. Her brow feels too hot. It's steamy inside our prison box, but when I check my own forehead, I know hers is hotter.

"Does anyone have water?" I ask.

There are no replies. I'm not surprised that we have all used up our small ration. "Soon," I say to Zuwida. "I'm sure we'll be there soon."

As I crawl back to sit against the side of the truck, I notice that the unscarved ones have once again separated themselves from the rest of us. They're huddled in a corner near the cab. We have our luggage with us now. I have chosen to sit on mine. They've opened theirs. Hawa is mostly shielded by the other two, but I see flashes of red, and I'm certain she's changing her clothes. Now Rayida holds a mirror for her, and I wonder what more she thinks she can do to hide the dirt and stink of us. And why she bothers. For Ushi? For a grand reception?

I'm worried. I take my notebook and pencil from my bag. *Mikray,* I write. *Be careful. The scarless ones heard your talk of escape. I don't trust them. They might tell if they think it buys them favor.*

I pass the note into Mikray's hand. There's a flash of anger as she reads the message. She turns her head toward Hawa, and I see her eyes widen, then slowly narrow as her face hardens. She looks confused. I wish we could talk, but it might be dangerous. Wrong, still, to trust those around us.

I force my face into its "sweet" expression and pretend to know nothing and see nothing. Only the smog-covered skyline of the vast city we're being driven through. I can see the tops of tall buildings though the high, small windows in the doors. And endless tall cranes like giant skeletons in the sky, working to make more tall buildings. The smell of burning coal grows worse. My lungs have been filled from time to time with sand and dust from the desert, and now

I wonder what breathing in coal dust will do to them. I'm certain the black smoke I see billowing from tall chimneys is not good to breathe; the air smells sharp and sulfurous.

As I watch, we pass lower and lower buildings. Some stretches of sky have no buildings at all. The Sichuanese man drives on and on—at least I think it is he who drives. I assume Ushi is riding in the cab of the truck with him. I don't know for certain.

Rubbing my white jade piece calms my body, if not my mind.

Eleven

THE TRUCK STOPS, the doors are thrown open, and there is Ushi. There's almost relief in that. One familiar thing. She watches as we jump down from our box. She seems as amazed as we are when the princesses emerge. Hawa has on a sleeveless red blouse, the top buttons undone to reveal an immodest amount of cleavage. What little skirt there is hangs from her hips, tight and short. Her legs are bare and amazingly long and slender. Her shoes are red-strapped wedges. Obviously she's forgotten that the distance from the floor of the truck to the ground will be the same getting out as it was getting in. She looks. She removes her shoes. And jumps. I almost applaud as she slides the shoes back on. It's a shame her performance is wasted on the likes of us and Ushi.

Rayida and the third girl of the scarfless trio, whose name I've learned is Nadia, follow in skirts not quite as short, heels not quite as high. They must believe that high fashion is the appropriate dress for the Surplus Work Force's arrival at our job. I can't help staring at Hawa as we're escorted to the entrance of a large three-story building.

The factory looks like an old warehouse—out here

along the road in a town with no tall buildings. Alongside it are abandoned storefronts with unlit neon signs. Broken sidewalks lead to warrens of dilapidated brick houses wrapped in a jungle of green vines. Most of the town seems to lie on the other side of the highway, across from the factory.

Like the truck, the building is in disrepair, but the sign painted on the front in bright blue announces HUBEI WORK WEAR COMPANY in bold, shiny new lettering.

Ushi leads us into a huge room filled with stacks of large cardboard boxes. Some are on movable racks, some piled deep against the outer walls. I expect many of the boxes will soon be given a ride in the truck that just delivered us. Ushi talks to a boy pushing one of the racks. He leaves. We're left standing. I see Zuwida weaving. Struggling to stay upright.

"May we have some water, please?" I ask Ushi.

"No," she says, and starts pacing, looking anxiously toward the door at the far end of the room. I wonder what her role is here at the factory. Maybe her job is done and she'll disappear.

A young man bursts in. Walks briskly toward us. "Welcome, welcome," he says over and over, in Mandarin, with a little bow of his head each time. He smiles as if he's pleased to see us. He is wearing a casual short-sleeved shirt with the collar unbuttoned and his undershirt showing through. His hair is cut as short as his clipped words. "Mr. Lee, general manager," he says, and bows again. "We are a new company with a good reputation for high-quality products and best services." He stops to smile, moving his gaze along the line, perhaps to make sure we're listening. He blinks twice as his eyes pass Hawa. He resets his smile and clears his throat. "We hold ourselves and our employees to the highest standards and expect nothing short of full dedication and the finest attention to work from you who have the privilege of working here."

I dare not look at Mikray, but I'm next to her and I shove my leg against hers. "Don't say anything," I hiss without moving my lips. She hears me. I don't know if she can hold back, but I know it's important. This man smiles too much. He's not to be trusted.

He treats us to a few banal statements about his talents and successes. His is a small special-order business, manufacturing custom-made work wear. Then he says again that we're expected to uphold his superior standards and informs us that we are to do everything Ushi tells us. With a curt bow and another glance at Hawa, he turns. Ushi applauds, so we all applaud until he disappears through the door.

He has not thanked Ushi for delivering us. He has not thanked us for giving up a year of our lives to help him. Ushi, who will continue to rule our lives, says nothing. We follow her through a door across the room from Mr. Lee's exit. We go up two long flights of stairs and come to a ceiling-high metal gate. Ushi takes a key from her pocket. Unlocks the gate. Sends us through. Locks it again behind her, and we continue up another flight of stairs to the top floor of the building. We turn right and pass the open door of the kitchen. Two women are inside, chopping and stirring. They look up as we pass. "We need a glass of water, please. Can we get it now?" I say this to Ushi, but it's loud enough for the women to hear. One of them stops what she is doing and heads for the sink.

"You'll have time later. Let's go," Ushi says, herding us down the hallway.

They cut my head off just to test the sharpness of a sword. I don't know why a line from a poem about torture passes through my mind right now. But I begin to wonder if we'll be allowed to eat any of the chicken I smell cooking in the pots on the stove.

I concentrate on the dingy walls, the rough-poured concrete floor of the hallway that takes us past a number of closed doors.

Ushi opens a door near the end of the hall, and we walk into a cramped, narrow, airless room. There are three metal bunk beds, crammed end to end, on each side. A clock sits on the sill of the window at the far end. If nothing else, we are to get to work on time. A bare light bulb hangs from the ceiling.

The princesses rush in to claim the bunks near the window. Adile streaks by and claims another bottom space. "Zuwida must have a lower bunk," she says. I drop everything and run to the bed next to her at the same time Patime and Letipe arrive. I turn and stick my arms out to block them. "Zuwida, come. This is *your* bed," I say. "Adile will be next to you if you need help during the night." I stand there with my arms thrust out, glaring at the girls. They gaze at me with stricken faces; the voice that came out of me is not one I recognize.

"Roshen," Patime says, "we want Zuwida to have a lower bed too. She should not have to climb a ladder, and it will be good if Adile can be right next to her. We weren't thinking of that when we rushed over. You could have asked nicely if we minded."

I stand as if paralyzed, my arms frozen in that awful gesture, my face so stiff and ugly I can't speak.

"What's going on here?" Ushi hollers as she moves toward us. "I don't know what your problem is, but it's time for rule number one. And listen good. The only language spoken here in this factory is Mandarin. If I hear anything else, or if one of the other workers reports that you're speaking"—she throws her hands in the air—"whatever language it is you speak, you'll be given points. Each point you're given deducts money from your pay. Get it? Mandarin only."

My arms slide down. I look at Patime and our eyes connect. *I'm sorry,* I mouth in Uyghur.

Ushi grabs my arm. "That's not Mandarin. Two words. Two points." She heads for the door.

"Follow me," she says. "Your tour isn't over."

I'm the last to leave. I see that Mikray has put my

luggage with hers on the bunk near the door. How many points for sneaking out? Where would we possibly go?

The door across from our room leads to two pit-toilet stalls. There's one large sink. "See that water spigot?" Ushi points to a pipe with a faucet on the end that sticks out into the room. "That's hot water. You'll wait in line like everyone else to get it. And you may not wash your clothes or hair at the spigot. That's what the pails are for." She walks over to a table to show us piles of peach-colored plastic pails stacked underneath.

On top of the table, piled high, are several stacks of enamel bowls. "The bowls are for food. Take one with you at mealtime. Wash it. Return it to the pile when you're through. You'll drink from them too, until we get more cups."

She takes one from the pile. Goes to the sink. Fills it. Turns. She heads toward Zuwida. "Take this and go lie down, before you collapse on the floor." She shakes her head as if she's being forced to give water to a stray dog. "I don't know why they sent *you*."

There are stairs at this end of the building with no gate to keep us locked in. I make a mental note. I'm sure Mikray is doing this too. The big boss, Mr. Lee, came and went from this end. His office is here somewhere. Maybe other important people are here too. Do they sleep here? No answers yet, just questions.

We go down one flight. Still no locked gate. *Interesting,*

I think. Maybe they reason that no one would dare to sneak past Big Boss.

Ushi points out a toilet room here on the second floor, then takes us into a huge space, almost the size of the whole building. This is where drudges like us work, all in one room. There must be almost fifty girls in this stifling hot, windowless cavern. Bare light bulbs hang from the high ceiling. Clever, the windowless room; we won't know whether it's day or night. Bodies bend over large tables, sit at oversize sewing machines. I can't tell what's happening at the far end of the room.

The smell of sweat and stale air overwhelms me. Soon we will be here too.

The girls nearby take a quick peek at us and go right back to work. We don't look like them. They all seem to be Chinese, about our age. Aren't they curious, at least about Hawa and her entourage? Or maybe they get points for looking away from their work. Ushi might see them, and she knows all about giving points.

"Three main jobs here," Ushi says. "Cutting, sewing, finishing. Your assignments will be posted on the wall. One of the girls in your section will train you. Work starts at seven." She stops and actually looks at us rather than at the floor, the ceiling, or the blank walls. She gives us her big smile, the one that shows all her teeth. "Guess what happens if you're late?"

She starts walking again. "And don't talk when you're

on the floor. You don't talk, you don't sing. You work." I can't resist humming to myself as I follow her. It helps me bear the knowledge that for one year I will be trapped in this room making work wear for the benefit of Mr. Lee—and our new Chinese cadre back in Hotan, who is "watching over" my family and Ahmat.

Halfway across we come to a large elevator. Two young men are loading boxes onto a wooden platform. There are ropes and pulleys for them to use when they lower the platform to the main floor. For a moment I try to imagine what was here in the warehouse before it became a factory. Maybe bags of rice or cotton that wouldn't have minded the heat, that would have given off a sweeter scent than our sweaty human bodies.

After we pass the sewing machines and other strange kinds of machinery, we come to what must be the "finishing" part. The girls here are ironing, stitching, folding. Gulnar, our embroiderer, may be the only one who gets a job she likes, serving out her time with a needle and thread.

I'm wrong about the girls not looking at us. They're just clever at not getting caught. What they don't try to hide is how they feel about us. "Hate" and "scorn" are words that come to mind. Do they even know who we are, that we're Uyghur and have been forced to come here? Or are we cheap labor brought in, taking jobs away from Chinese girls who want them? I've heard that many Chinese farm girls who want to leave home and work in the cities are denied permits. Why are they going to all the trouble of bringing us here if there are plenty of people to do the jobs?

I know the answer—the quotas our cadres are forced to fill. The Chinese girls probably don't know about quotas. I can't blame them for hating us.

We climb the stairs to the third floor again. The smell of chicken is more powerful than ever. Even Ushi thinks about food. "Breakfast is served at six thirty," she says.

Rayida sidles up to her. "Will we have supper tonight?" she asks in a pathetic voice.

Ushi rolls her eyes. "Supper's handed out at seven, at the end of the day shift. Bring your dishes to the kitchen.

"And, by the way, from now on no headscarves. Am I clear? Not in the toilets, not in the hallways, not in the factory, not in your room." She keeps walking, although most of us have stopped. Stunned. Why have we been allowed to wear them all this time if it's against the rules? Even back home we had to remove our scarves in the classrooms. Ushi let us wear them just long enough for everyone here to know we are "other," not like them. People that their government wants to get rid of. Surplus Work Force really means Surplus People. People who do not deserve respect. How naïve I was to believe we might be spared this humiliation. Our heads must be uncovered. The tradition that my people have practiced for centuries to fulfill God's commandment for modesty is unwelcome at Hubei Work Wear Company. We're now under Ushi's commandments.

With no further words, Ushi leaves us. We go to our room. Zuwida is curled up on her bunk, sleeping. Her bed has been made and her head rests on a soft pillow. A hush pervades the room as we each go to our respective bunks. Mikray stands by ours. I claim the upper bunk as mine. Laid out on the slab of plywood that is my bed is a folded sheet, a blanket, a towel, and a blue smock—the uniform the girls downstairs were wearing.

"How did Zuwida's bed get made?" I ask Mikray, in Uyghur. If someone wants to report me for not speaking Mandarin, let them. "And she has a pillow." Mikray shrugs as we both look over at Zuwida, who is sleeping peacefully. I believe she will get well if she gets a bit of care.

———

Three hours later a bell clangs and rumbles through the building like a strung-out thunderclap.

Then silence.

The building stops humming as the drone of whirling and whizzing machines ends. A stampede of footsteps hits the stairs. It's food time. In spite of our hunger, and by consensus, we do not rush to be first in line ahead of the fifty or so girls we saw working downstairs. We stand and wait.

A blur of blue smocks invades the hallway, then turns at the toilet room. There's no way everyone can fit in. They don't. A line forms out into the hallway. I'm afraid to even imagine what the rules are about peeing in the downstairs toilet room during work hours.

When it appears that everyone has left to go to the kitchen, we go into the toilet room and pick up our bowls —eleven of us. Zuwida cannot be roused.

The doors in the hallway have been opened. I peek in. Girls are already sitting on beds eating, in rooms that are as stark and crowded as ours—and littered with clothes draped over the bed rails. Boxes and bags and peach-colored pails are strewn all over the floor. We've been neat, storing our clothes, everything, under the bunks in our suitcases. I hope we Uyghur girls will keep some sense of pride in how we live.

We join the end of the line with our empty bowls. Others pass when they leave the kitchen with their bowls filled. They say nothing, just stare at us with no attempt to hide their disdain.

A girl passes with her head in the air, her fingers pinching her nose. "We don't smell like migrants," Mikray says. "You do." She says it loud enough for a dozen or so girls to hear, and I think they might have thrown their food in her face if they hadn't been hungry.

"Don't pay any attention to her," Hawa says in an imperious tone, going up to the girl. Hawa looks over her shoulder at Mikray, shrugs, then leans over and whispers something to the girl. The girl looks at Mikray and laughs. She nods at Hawa, then gestures to those around her, and they move on.

Hawa turns and walks up to Mikray. "That was stupid," she says quietly in Uyghur. "We have to be here for a year. I want to eat and have some kind of life. Don't ruin it for all of us." She moves back to her place in line.

Mikray's chest heaves. I think she might explode, but she stands rooted to the floor. She heard Hawa, and maybe she knows her outburst was unwise. We have no friends here, no place of safety. We're at the mercy of Boss Lee and Ushi. We have no one to run to.

"You're too important to us to waste energy on small things, Mikray," I say. "We need your wisdom for what's ahead. Be clever for us. Your power is in your cunning."

———

Being last in line was not a good idea. Perhaps the cook wasn't told there would be twelve more to feed. She ladles yellow rice into our bowls and covers it with a watery broth that has a few flecks of chicken in it. At least it has no smell of pork.

The cook, too, looks at us as if we smell. Her nose scrunches up into her face. We have, in fact, used the time we were waiting to sponge-bathe in our buckets and to wash our hair—using the spigot one by one as someone stood watch by the door—knowing it might be the only time we'll ever be alone and able to do it. We have on clean clothes. We're less sweaty and dirty than she is here in her steamy kitchen, at least until the heat in our room, in this factory, in this part of China, boils us alive. The temperature is already higher than on any day I can remember, and the summer's just begun.

Zuwida stirs as we come back into the room to eat. "Please check her fever, Roshen," Adile says. I cradle her head in my hands and touch my forehead to hers. Her face is flushed but calm, her body less tense.

"Has your headache gone, Zuwida?" I whisper. She nods. "We have food. Would you like something to eat?"

"Just water. Please." Her words come slowly.

"I have something for you," I say. Adile holds her hand while I go to my bed and retrieve my water bottle. The empty water bottle I hid in my bag during our journey is now filled. It will be Zuwida's. Adile and I help her to drink. Her eyes flutter and she sinks again into a deep sleep —a peaceful sleep, as if some special potion is healing her mind and body. I guide her hand to the bottle. If she wakes and is thirsty, she will know it is there.

We eat, replace our bowls as ordered, and turn off the light.

I will sleep. What dream can my mind conjure that is more bleak and lonely than my life right now?

Twelve

Ushi has judged me sweet and harmless. She's entrusted me with a lethal weapon. I'm assigned to the cutting section, along with Nadia and Jemile, and given long, sharp scissors with thin blades. Excellent for cutting through the reams of material piled on the table in front of me—and perhaps other things.

For a moment I blank out. I don't hear the half Mandarin, half Sichuanese of my instructor assaulting my ear. I'm remembering the girl who said goodbye to her family and to Ahmat less than a week ago, someone who never would have thought of scissors as a deadly weapon, even in jest.

"Watch what you're doing!" my trainer yells in my ear. "If you can't cut a hammer loop without messing up, you don't belong here. You should at least be able to do that."

She's right. I should. I can. And I'm beginning to know what my new life will be. This piece of cloth, these scissors are the only things I must think about. There is no time for other thoughts, no time for dreaming. Two hundred and fifty hammer loops. Now. Fast.

One of the floor walkers, a little boss of some kind, comes over. She's heard the yelling above the roar of the machines. She says nothing. Just stands behind me. I'm lucky that anger steadies my hand. For a moment I do two things at once: I cut straight, precise lines, and I remember with pride that I was the honor student in my class.

Two hundred and fifty hammer loops done. Now I'm assigned left back pockets, which must have a slit for a button closure. The slit is to be three and one-half centimeters from the top of the pocket, allowing for the hem at the top; the slit itself is to be two and a quarter centimeters long. I am given a razor-sharp retractable blade to make the slit. Little Boss stands behind me while I cut and slice the first two pockets. The next 248 I am allowed to do on my own, apparently having passed her test.

My trainer stands next to me doing the same work, cutting pockets from the same coarse mud-colored material that I've been given. She's fast and accurate as she guides the scissors through the cloth. She works with a steady rhythm that I find myself following, a rhythm grounded in the tremble of the wooden table beneath the cloth as we crunch the heavy scissors.

Place pattern. *Crrrunch*, release; *crrrunch*, release along the bottom. *Crrrunch*, release, *crrrunch*, release; *crrrunch*, release along the side. Turn scissors. *Crrrunch*, release; *crrrunch*, release along the top. *Crrrunch*, release, *crrrunch*, release; *crrrunch* release along the side. Scissors down. Take razor. Make slit. Razor down. Remove pocket. Place in pile. Place pattern. *Crrrunch*, release, *crrrunch*, release . . .

No song or poem I know has this rhythm, so I can give

it no melody, but I find comfort in the repeat of the task. I beat the sequence with my toes to help relieve my tired legs. I'm not used to standing for so many hours.

Will I so quickly forget the rhythms of my own land, my own people, and give the new poems I write the rhythm of scissors? For a moment I stop cutting. I squeeze my eyes shut until I can see images of the farm, my family together, planting seeds, then harvesting our crops of carrots and beans and melons. At the end of these days, sitting together under a tree while Father plays his *dutar* and we share songs and stories before falling into a peaceful night's rest. Our rhythms. My memories. I must keep them alive.

Thwack! A metal rod hits my calves. Little Boss has been watching. I struggle to keep upright. I will not let her see my pain. My hand still holds the scissors. *Crrrunch,* release, *crrrunch,* release . . . Make button slit. Place pocket in pile. Begin again. Again. And again.

Next, the right back pocket, which is exactly the same as the left back pocket.

At right back pocket number 136, an earsplitting bell vibrates off the walls and through my body. There is a rush of people, yet no one in the cutting section moves. Then I understand why. Little Boss comes around with a basket, collecting scissors and razors. We are not to move until every dangerous weapon is picked up and accounted for. Perhaps I'm not the only one whose thoughts turn to transgression with a pair of scissors in my hands.

I pretend I'm not in pain as I climb the steps and wait

in line for the toilet and food. That takes fifteen minutes. It takes less than three minutes to eat watery cabbage soup. Now Mikray and I sit on her bed, holding empty bowls. We seem to have formed little groups. Hawa, Rayida, and Nadia huddle together by the window. Patime, Letipe, and Nurbiya sit on a bunk, saying little. Adile and Jemile attend to Zuwida. Only Gulnar sits alone on her upper bunk, working her needle and thread.

Mikray and I have a bit of privacy, sitting close to the door. "What happened?" I ask in Uyghur, pointing to her red, swollen hand. My hand is swollen too, only not as badly as Mikray's. I don't mention the welt on my leg.

"The rivet machine. I have to put rivets on the sides of every pocket and on loops, straps, any stress points." She looks down. "The handle is hard to press. It takes a lot of force." Then she laughs and moves closer. "It may be the best thing that's happened," she says. "The person training me is one of the young Chinese men we saw loading boxes on the elevator. When he's not doing that, he helps with the rivets. He likes to talk, so he pretends he's giving me instructions. And he gets away with it." She stops. Leans even closer. "Roshen, he lives nearby and goes home every night. I think he's the one who'll help me. If my hand and shoulder hurt, that's okay. I'll get used to it."

"No. If you're thinking about sneaking out, you can't do that. It's too dangerous. They'll punish you. You can't trust him—or anybody."

Mikray's face tightens. "We'll see," she says. "I have

unfinished business to take care of at home. I can't do it from inside this prison."

There can be no more talk. The other girls pass us now on their way to wash their bowls. Our half hour is almost up. I see that Zuwida is alone, curled like a little nestling bird, fast asleep. Gulnar stands beside her.

"Can't we let her sleep?" I whisper.

"She insists we wake her," Gulnar says. "She doesn't want to lose pay. She volunteered to come, Roshen, so she could earn money to send home."

We both look at the clock on the sill. It's almost one o'clock. Gulnar puts her hand on Zuwida's shoulder and gives her a gentle shake. "She works in finishing with Hawa and me. We help her. I think she'll be all right."

The clanging bell sends me on a dash to the sink and down the stairs to my place at the cutting table. After I receive scissors and a cutting razor, I finish 114 more right back pockets. They are taken away, and I am given a pattern for the left front swing pocket. Two hundred and fifty of these, and I am given the pattern for the right swing pocket. Then the right chest pocket with flap. Then the left chest pocket with pencil slot.

I act as though I have to use the toilet, which isn't true. We're allowed two six-minute breaks each day, and I see no reason not to take them. While Little Boss adds my name to the sign-out sheet on her desk, I sneak a glance at the production report she's working on. Each of us seems to be listed individually with a log of the work we've done.

That's why she herself collects the piles of pockets we cut. Are we paid by the numbers? A quarter of a yuan for each twenty pockets? That has not been mentioned and they only told Father that we would be paid. They wouldn't tell him how much. If I must be here, I want to make at least enough to help with my tuition and books for college. I head for the toilet.

Six minutes is a very short time. Even so, when I return, something has changed. Little Boss stands alongside her desk with rigid posture, her eyes looking straight ahead, unnatural and unblinking. I follow her gaze and see Big Boss walking down the aisle toward the sewing section. He stops at the desk of the sewing supervisor and picks up a paper. Nods. Moves on toward finishing. I wonder if he knows that Hawa is there ironing? Maybe he won't pay much attention to her after he sees her in her blue smock.

I go to my workstation before Little Boss can find me staring. She might recover from her ordeal—Big Boss obviously looked at her numbers too—and realize I've taken an extra minute, watching what's happening.

If the girls around me had their eyes half-closed from fatigue and boredom when I left, those eyes are now wide open, those fingers flying. I quicken my pace as much as I can. My hand is numb; I can no longer get a good grip on the scissors. Concentrate. *Think of nothing else,* I tell myself as I cut yet one more left chest pocket. Put the scissors down. Pick up the razor. Make the pencil slot. Put the razor down. Move the pocket to the pile. Place the pattern on the cloth. *Crrrunch*, release; *crrrunch*, release along the bottom . . .

Then it's as if a wave sweeps over the room. The machines are still making noise, but somehow I know that all the Chinese girls are holding their breath. Their heads are bent over their work, but their eyes watch Big Boss stride down the aisle and leave. My trainer reveals nothing to me, but I can tell from her tight lips and firm jaw that what just happened is not good.

It's not too long before Ushi comes into the room. She talks to Little Boss, who keeps bowing her head up and down. I wondered why we hadn't seen Ushi today, and guessed that she was given some time off. Now my wondering turns to fear that she might be Big Boss Number Two.

Ushi moves on toward sewing. Little Boss comes to the cutting tables to deliver the news that production is behind. "There will be no break for supper," she tells us. "You are to work until ten o'clock. Then you'll be fed. You'll have a short break for tea. Soon," she says.

Impulsively, I thrust my right hand toward her. By now it's puffed up and ugly, and obviously I can no longer hold a pair of scissors.

"You girls from the north are supposed to be good workers," she says. "That's what we were told." She jerks her head at me. "Don't look here for sympathy. I know how many pieces you've cut. It's because of people like you that we have to work overtime tonight." She turns and goes back to her desk where she . . . what? Sits and counts pieces and puts numbers on a sheet of paper?

I am now the most unpopular person in the cutting section—probably actively despised. Jemile and Nadia, my Uyghur cutting companions, may still be supportive, especially if their scissors hands are as sore as mine.

I become left-handed. I'm awkward and slower than a snail, but I'm trying. I keep a determined look on my face.

Tea break is a tiny paper cup filled with tepid tea, delivered on a cart by one of the boys. We're supposed to drink fast and return the cup to the cart as he whizzes by. I think it might be an unusual kindness until I taste it. It's more than tea. A stimulant of some kind must have been put into it to keep us awake and make us more productive, and I've already swallowed it. I don't like being tricked, but it wasn't just me, it was everyone on the floor. Didn't they know? Or maybe they like taking drugs.

I force myself to think of left chest pockets with pencil slots. When 250 are done, Little Boss throws me the pattern for patches that are to be sewn onto the inside of a pant leg to hold a kneepad.

The slight raise of a shoulder sends an alert around the cutting tables as Ushi walks rapidly down the aisle, followed by the boy who brought us tea. Minutes later she comes back. The boy is carrying Zuwida's limp body in his arms. Her eyes are closed.

"No!" I cry. Now the stares are directed at me, and I go

back to work and pretend I didn't say anything. But I can think only of Zuwida and wonder what is happening.

It seems forever before it's ten o'clock. Jemile, Nadia, and I are closest to the door and the first to bolt up the stairs, ignoring Little Boss's shouts about waiting for scissor collection. We run to our room, and there is Zuwida in sleeping clothes, curled up on her bed. I touch her. Her face is flushed and hot, but she's alive. Sleeping. Sleeping peacefully. I find a note half-hidden under her pillow.

Adile reads the note with me. It's written in Mandarin. It says that Zuwida has been given broth and a special tea that should help her sleep and bring down her fever. *There is a thermos of hot water hidden under the bed and a packet of tea for her when she wakes. Please do not let her work tomorrow. I will see that she is taken care of.* The note isn't signed.

I go to the hallway to see if anyone is waiting there, watching—someone who might have helped. The girls have returned. I see no one who could have been filled with such kindness.

Thirteen

AFTER DAYS AND days of mud-colored cloth and working overtime, I arrive in the morning to find bolts of blue material. We spend the day cutting short sleeves, hundreds and hundreds of short sleeves. The cloth is not as coarse and heavy as the mud-colored one; it's easier to cut through. By now my hand has become stronger, although calluses have not yet formed over the most tender spots.

Instead of our suppertime delivery of energy tea, Big Boss shows up. I know without looking that he's in the doorway. We all know. He has a power that stills us in his presence. We put our scissors down. The din from the sewing machines decrescendos to complete silence, followed by a loud thud that has to be Mikray slamming down the handle to implant one last rivet.

In the awed silence that comes over us, Big Boss makes his way to the freight elevator, where Ushi and the three little bosses rush to his side. The handymen and kitchen workers stand in the doorway. Ushi is all smile and teeth, which can mean anything, but generally not good news. Big Boss's face is covered with smile and teeth too, not nearly as impressive as Ushi's. Everyone else looks nervous.

"Hubei Work Wear has once again proven its high

standards in producing customized, quality work wear. My reputation for excellence is preserved, and the order will be delivered on time. A satisfied customer is my greatest achievement." Big Boss preens. His hand sweeps the air. He goes on and on about his company's greatness and his own greatness. His ambitions for even more greatness. My legs ache from having to stand and hear more and more about his greatness.

At last we get some news. We are to be paid the wages we earned and to have a day off. Ushi will fill in the details. Big Boss leaves, and Ushi, still smiling, steps into his place. Ushi *is* Big Boss Number Two.

"There will be no work assignments tomorrow. It's a vacation day for which you will *not* be paid," she announces. A sign-out sheet will be monitored at the main door from six o'clock in the morning on. The curfew for return is nine o'clock at night. Triple points for each minute late.

———

There is no bell this morning. Even so, we wake early and stand in line for watery porridge. The line is shorter than usual. Girls who live nearby left earlier to catch buses, all they'd talked about since the announcement. Many of the Chinese girls live too far away for a day trip, so they chat about shopping, going to a park. They whisper about a factory that may be hiring, a job that pays more. They'll try for an interview, or at least leave their names.

We, the Uyghur girls, got a special talk from Ushi right

after Big Boss's speech. Don't bother to stand in line for the paymaster, she said. We still owe the company money for our transportation to get here, for food, for uniforms, and on and on. Then she told us we were too naïve to roam about, and no one was available to go with us, and we were probably too tired to want to go anyway. Was I too dazed to protest? Mikray's rivet-machine friend has given her the name of an illicit—"black"—café that would allow us to get on the internet without special ID. Finally I'd be able to get a message to Ahmat. And I stood there—mute. I didn't say a word. Nor did anyone else, not even Mikray. Ushi had disappeared by the time I woke to reality.

———

It's bad to have a day of rest. Good for the body, bad for the mind. Words of a Uyghur poem creep into my head. Father taught me these words, and we talked about how brave the poet was to write something that landed him in jail. I say the poem to myself over and over. *Wake up!* the poet tells me.

> *If you do not open your eyes and look about,*
> *You will die asleep one day, that is your fate.*

I have looked about, and I said nothing when robbed of a day off! I've let them abuse me, work me until I can't stand up any longer, feed me rotten, bug-infested soup— and I do nothing for myself. Doesn't the poet know I have no choice if I want to see Ahmat again? My family? I can be taken away to one of the government's hidden prisons for "reeducation" if I try to escape or fight for fair treatment. It doesn't take much to be "disappeared," and Ushi doesn't like troublemakers.

Besides, I tell myself, I'm only here for a year, and I'm not dying. Bad food, long hours, meanness, and bullying don't end your life. If I keep out of trouble, I can go home. The words of another poet are meant for me now.

> *I am the traveler ...*
> *The newest Gypsy—*
> *Wandering around the world,*
> *Finding my way home*
> *Whether in snow or rain.*

I'll get home again and live the life I've planned. That's what I choose to do. I'll count cut sleeves and pockets and hammer loops by the hundreds to keep from going mad, to keep from thinking. And I'll silence the voices of the poets who ask too much of me.

I dream when I should do laundry. Sweat drips on the sheet I could be washing. Instead I stare out the window at the putrid smog that fills the air and my lungs. I long for the sand-filled air that sometimes blows across the desert and seeps through the cracks in the walls. That air would let me know I am home with Ahmat. But I'm *not* with Ahmat. I can only write more love poems and pretend.

When all the rest have finished their cleaning frenzy, and drying clothes are draped over every available bed frame and doorknob, I clamber down the rails of my bunk, collect a few dirty garments, and hobble on my achy, swollen legs to the toilet room.

There are just a few drops of soap left in the plastic bottle I stole from the garbage, so I launder only one peach-colored bucket's worth. I'm on my knees kneading and squeezing, more fiercely than necessary because I'm angry at myself for not having packed soap, when Jemile drops down beside me. "Roshen, I need a favor," she whispers. Her head is hung, her face flushed. And then she doesn't speak. I wait. She squats there, miserable, and I'm angry because we're all miserable and I don't need to be more depressed.

"Okay, Jemile. What?" I say, and she flinches. "Just tell me. Come on. Of course I'll help."

Still nothing. I wring out the blue smock. Throw it on the pile beside me and grab a handful of dirty underwear. "I can't help if I don't know what you want."

Our eyes meet as she backs away. Pain twists her face.

I reach out. Touch her. Her body freezes. I try to wrap my arms around her and hold her. She pushes me away.

"He . . . touched . . . me," she finally whispers.

"Who, Jemile? Who touched you?"

"A man . . . in the toilets. Please don't let me be alone there again," she pleads. "Please go with me." The words begin to tumble out. "And . . . I can't go home now. They won't want me. He . . . he grabbed my breast. Put his hand under my panties. Then I bit him and he let go and hit me and I ran away. But he'll try again, I know," she says.

She turns her beautiful, innocent, unguarded face to me. "Why would he do that?" she asks.

My arms reach out to enfold her.

At home we are protected by our families, by our Uyghur boys. Touching, all touching, is an intimacy reserved for marriage. The almost kiss I exchanged with Ahmat sealed our bond forever.

"You'll never have to be alone again, Jemile," I say when her body calms. "When you need to go to the toilet, walk by and I'll follow you. We'll go together from now on. And Jemile . . ." I stroke her brow, smooth her hair, for she is now my little sister and I'll protect her with any power I still possess. "His touch has not destroyed your purity. This awful man wanted to harm you, and you fought and got away, my little Jemile. You have nothing to be ashamed of. Remember only that he struck you. That he hurt you." I pull her more tightly to me. "It will be our secret," I say.

I make her look at me. Let our eyes hold until I see her trust.

"Now, do you have dirty clothes? Have you done your laundry?" She shakes her head.

There is comfort in washing clothes together. I've acquired a shadow, one I welcome. One who will let me hold her and comfort her as I try to heal myself.

After lunch I half sleep, half entertain myself by watching the action around me, which helps to keep my mind off the words of the poet who expects me to "wake up" and the oppressively hot, steamy, unbearable weather. Gulnar's needle moving in and out of her embroidery lulls me, as it must in some way calm whatever thoughts are in her head. Jemile and Adile talk quietly to Zuwida, who rests on her slab of plywood. It seems to have acquired a thin mattress over the last few days. Her mysterious guardian has done well for her. In fact, I see a hint of color on Zuwida's face, a sign of health that wasn't there before. She's returned to work; there are stories of Hawa helping by ironing some of Zuwida's allotment as well as her own.

Hawa. She amuses me. Oblivious, it seems, to the squalid surroundings we live in. She huddles now with Rayida and Nadia as they take turns looking in a mirror, painting their eyes in different colors and shapes as if they're movie stars.

It's not long before the pile of still-unwashed clothes at the foot of my bunk invades my consciousness. I climb down the bunk frame, wondering about the usefulness of a soapless wash. And wondering where Mikray is. I thought she was sleeping. I gather my clothes, go to the toilet room. Mikray's not there. I stuff my clothes into a bucket and go looking.

She's not in the hallway. I check the gate at the bottom of the stairs by the kitchen. It's locked. I go to the stairs at the other end of the hallway. No one is around. I sneak to the second floor, try the factory door. It's locked. The toilet room is empty. There are other doors and rooms, but why would Mikray be hiding? From what? Maybe she snuck out when the guard wasn't looking. It will be harder to sneak back in.

Will she come back?

And why am I sneaking around looking for her? She got me into trouble and I'm the one who got caught!

I hang my second batch of laundry so that it covers part of Mikray's bunk and then sit there myself with my notebook and pen. Maybe it won't look quite so empty when people pass by — Mikray might be sleeping in the shadow of the hanging laundry. I don't want anyone to ask me where she is.

Around suppertime the Chinese girls begin to come back. There are questioning looks when we line up for food. Hawa keeps looking at me; I'm usually with Mikray. I meet her eyes, give my head a quick shake. She turns away, and somehow I'm sure she knows Mikray is gone. Others begin to notice.

I eat the disgusting food that's ladled into my bowl, wash the bowl, and return to Mikray's bunk. We've been speaking Uyghur all day, which has put everyone in a more hopeful mood. No one talks about Mikray. A worried glance now and then. A shrug.

The chatter and excitement in the hallway grows to a high level as the rest of the Chinese girls return with tales of their day. After the nine o'clock deadline, Ushi patrols the hallway. It quiets down.

Gulnar puts away her embroidery. We fold our clean clothes. We're settling in for the night when Ushi shows up for a rare visit. Until tonight she's taken little interest in what we do on the third floor. She starts counting and ends up with her eyes on Mikray's empty bunk. "Where's that one?" she barks.

"In the toilet," I answer.

She humphs. Leaves.

"Is it all right if I turn out the light?" I ask. There are nods of agreement.

A few minutes later I climb down. Pull my suitcase out from under the bunk. Remove most of my clothes, arrange them on the top bunk, and cover them with a sheet, so it looks as if a person is lying there asleep. I curl up on the lower bunk, facing the wall, and pull the sheet around my head.

After it's totally dark in the hallway, I hear a shuffle of feet. A beam of light passes over my body. Holds for a few seconds. Moves on. The feet shuffle away.

Fourteen

THERE ARE NOISES in the hallway. My eyes pop open. It's daylight and I'm still in Mikray's bed! I slide out and climb to the top bunk. I don't know what Mikray's done, where she is, but I know that if she's caught, the authorities will take her away and she might never be heard from again.

I won't be taken down with her!

But there's someone in my bed. Mikray is sound asleep, smelling like kitchens and naan. I squeeze her arm hard. "Get in your own bed. Quickly," I hiss.

She springs up. "Okay, okay," she whispers. "I'm going." She avoids looking at me as she scrambles over the rail and settles on the lower bunk.

She's put my clothes into two neat piles. Hidden in one pile is a small round of naan in a paper wrapping. I can't believe she did this and I didn't wake up. Our bed squeaks when we move.

I lie down and try to pretend nothing has happened, but it's hard to pretend that ten pairs of eyes have not witnessed what just went on. I see some shaking of heads. It's hard for anyone to understand what goes on in Mikray's mind—and in mine, too, since I was willing to risk my life covering for her. If Ahmat's warning proves to be right, if there's an informer among us, will she report Mikray or both of us?

The noise in the hallway grows, and there's a collective surge out of bed so that we can claim our space in the toilet room before the others take over. Mikray is sound asleep again, so I leave her on her own.

It's time to line up for breakfast. Mikray is still sleeping, and I want to leave her there—let her get points for being late for work—but I don't. I shake her. "Time for breakfast. We have work today, you know," I say, and leave.

I ate the naan, every crumb of it, yet here I am. It seemed to make me hungrier than ever. I crave food, any food.

Mikray's at the back of the line when I pass with my scoop of watery porridge and go to our room to eat. I sit on her bunk because it would be odd if I didn't. No one climbs to an upper bunk with food. When she comes to sit next to me, I take a good look at her. She pulls her forehead so tight that her brows almost meet and her eyes are scary, way beyond anger.

I'm sorry I've been mean. I reach out, lay my hand on her shoulder. "Mikray, we must talk. I don't know how we'll do that, but we must find a time." I whisper this in Uyghur. "Thank you for the naan. Will you be all right today?"

She doesn't answer, or look at me, but tears well in her eyes. Her hand goes up to cover mine, and I'm ashamed.

My troubles are missing Ahmat and my family. I'm loved, pampered. Naïve. What has Mikray's life been like?

———

I'm waiting for the tap on my shoulder. Little Boss will come behind me. Tap. I'll lay down my scissors and quietly follow her. Mikray might already be in Ushi's office. If she's not, it probably means they want to get my side of the story first so they can catch her in double lies, then give her double prison time—or disappear her forever. I wonder how long they'll disappear me for? Is my crime as bad as Mikray's?

At 250 blue pockets I'm still at the cutting table. To distract myself, I go through the list of Uyghur girls again, one by one, trying to decide who might be the traitor. I'm always left with Gulnar, but only because she stays aloof, always embroidering, pensive. I sense, though, that she suffers a deep sorrow and has no interest in betrayal. Perhaps it's enough that forty-eight Chinese girls and little and big bosses are free to report our disloyalties and misdeeds any time they like, and Mikray was clever enough to escape unnoticed.

My thoughts change when it's announced that the "blue" job we just began will require overtime. That's how Big Boss manages business, we've heard the Chinese girls say. He gets new customers by promising fast delivery and has no problem making people work until they get sick or find another job and leave. That must be why Ushi brought us here. Big Boss can count on us. We're indentured for a year.

When our year is up, will Ushi take us back home or say goodbye, good luck, and lock us out? Maybe they think the pretty, happy Uyghur girls love to cut and sew and iron so much they'll stay and help make Big Boss wealthy.

At my 267th front swing pocket, Jemile passes by. I nod, give her time to sign out, then write my name in Little Boss's book and follow her. There's no way to be sneaky about it; sooner or later Little Boss will pay attention. For now Jemile and I enjoy our allotted six minutes. We do our business, then stretch our fingers, massage each other's hands.

For some reason I look up—and see something I'm sure wasn't there before. There's a little box high on the wall above the sink. It rotates slowly back and forth. It's a surveillance camera. They're recording everything we say and do in the toilet room.

I shift so my back is to it and put my finger on my lips while I jabber away, saying any nonsense that comes into my mind. Between the jabber I whisper what I've seen. "Don't look," I warn her. "Don't let them know we've seen it—and there may be more all over. Okay," I say in my normal voice, "one more stretch, then . . ." I stop, realizing I'm speaking Uyghur. "Back to work," I say as cheerfully as I can in Mandarin. "More blue pockets."

We've been recorded speaking Uyghur. We've just lost a lot of points.

And so much more.

We're already in prison! We're locked in *and* they spy on us.

Hey, poor Uyghur, wake up, that is enough sleep. . . .
Stand up! I tell you. Raise your head, wake up from your
dream.

I'm haunted by this poem. Father knows the danger in passing on the songs and poems of our people. To be caught with this poem in your home is a crime. Why did he teach it to me?

———

I've given up counting pockets. Now I watch people go to and come back from the toilet room. I can tell which ones have discovered the little black box. It's not easy to cut perfect pockets and keep up with this distraction, but hopefully the challenge will help to keep me sane and awake. A toilet break is a big deal for us. Twice a day, if no one else is in the stalls, we've been speaking Uyghur. We've said things we shouldn't. That's all over now.

It's late afternoon when I see Mikray going to the sign-out desk. *Please, Mikray, be careful,* I say silently. I can't follow her. I must save my second sign-out for Jemile.

Finally, in the late-night supper line, I stand next to Mikray. We're surrounded by our own kind. After checking for little black boxes rotating back and forth on the walls of the hallway and finding none, I tell Mikray about the surveillance device. Her upper lip tightens. She lowers her head, curls her hands into fists. After a moment she nods and looks up. "I didn't know," she says. "Thank you."

"Mikray, why did you sneak out? If I hadn't helped you, you would have been caught." I'm becoming expert at talking—hissing—with my teeth clenched so no one can tell I'm saying anything. My expression, too, is one of sweetness, like *wasn't it fun today, cutting a zillion pockets?*

She looks right at me now. Her question shows in her eyes.

"Yeah," I say. "Ushi checked on us after curfew. You weren't there. She came back after the lights were out. I thought she might. That's why I was in your bed." Every word brings me closer to explosion. "You could have gotten all of us into trouble. Especially me!"

Mikray closes her eyes. She won't let me look in. She turns and goes down the hall. I let her go. Let *her* go hungry if she wants to. I'm not willing to do that.

It's a long wait for food. By the time I get back to our room with my bowl, Mikray is curled up on her bed. Asleep? Maybe. I sit with Zuwida and Adile and Jemile.

I get ready for bed and climb to my bunk. There is a note for me, in Uyghur.

> *Roshen,*
>
> *Thank you for helping me. I had intended to return before curfew, but something went wrong. I'll have to leave again. I'll know how to plan better next time. I have to get in touch with my mother, but I couldn't contact her. That's all I can say.*
>
> *Please tear this note up and flush it away. I don't want anyone here to get in trouble for my sake.*
>
> *I hope I won't need your help again.*
>
> *Mikray*

Fifteen

THERE IS A HUGE BLACK CLOUD passing by our window that will soon deluge the earth with more rain and saturate our steam box of a room with more sogginess. "Unleash your winds, your thunder and lightning, almighty gods of black clouds!" I cry out—in Mandarin. A few of the girls who aren't too busy sweating and falling asleep over their bowls look at me and grin. *And may your lightning strike dead the workmen in the toilet room,* I mouth in Uyghur as I point across the hallway.

Surveillance devices are being installed in the upstairs toilet room. We were given the privilege of observing the workmen with their wires and drills as we rushed into the room to relieve ourselves at the start of lunch break. There is still no sign of a device in our room, but we've decided there must be hidden microphones somewhere. We mostly speak Mandarin and only whisper or mouth Uyghur.

Suddenly Ushi sweeps into our room and shuts the door, which we have been commanded to keep open always. I'm sure she heard what I just said and is about to exact punishment. All eyes swivel back and forth between Ushi and me.

"We are being inspected by the company that is purchasing the coveralls we're currently making," Ushi says, her head stuck high in the air, her big mouth working. "They're touring the factory floor and will be asking questions. You, however, are not to answer them." She pauses and levels her eyes at us. "They've been told that you belong to a tribe that does not speak Mandarin. If any one of you answers or shows the slightest indication that you understand them, there will be consequences . . . you can't begin to imagine." She smiles. I'm certain it will be something more than points. "Do you understand?" She pauses again. No one says anything. She turns and leaves.

It is a moment before any of the "tribe" moves, not until Adile calls out that we'll be late for work. We rush to clean our bowls and run down the stairs. Losing pay for being late is something we don't do. Playing dumb in front of the people who are buying the blue coveralls we're making is a new test. One I would take pleasure in failing, but I think this is not the showdown to have—if we ever do have one.

"I'll smile sweetly, Ushi," I say to a pocket and keep on cutting.

It is nearly time for our late-afternoon energy tea when Big Boss, Ushi, and two men who are not Chinese come onto the factory floor. The men are nicely dressed in business suits and ties. They're ushered along our cutting tables and stop in front of one of the more comely and quiet Chinese girls who works nearby.

"The men would like to ask you some questions," Ushi

says. The girl seems a bit scared, but she puts down her scissors and folds her hands. Her eyes look straight ahead, not at the men.

One of the men, who speaks in schoolboy Mandarin, asks her to describe her workday. The girl answers in a singsong voice about breakfast, work, lunch, work, then dinner and quiet evenings spent chatting with friends. "Do you ever have to work overtime?" he asks.

"Oh, now and then," she says.

"Will you have to work late tonight?"

The girl's eyes flick back and forth, trying to look at Ushi without seeming to. Has Ushi forgotten to ply her with all the possible answers? She finally shakes her head in a halfhearted way as she looks down at the floor.

It's hard to suppress a laugh. For some reason the whole thing amuses me. I should be plotting to throw rotten potato soup in Ushi's face when we finally are given something to eat at ten o'clock tonight, or eleven, or whenever they decide.

The men in suits have stopped in front of me. They're speaking English. I studied English in school and know some of the words. No, I know all the words if I concentrate. They're surprised that foreigners work here; they want to know more about me. It's obvious that Big Boss and Ushi don't understand what the men say in English. The men have just said that I'm pretty, and when I shoot a quick glance at my bosses, they have no reaction, just keep looking ramrod stiff. I'm blushing and I don't know how to hide it. To stop it.

The men speak Mandarin again. They ask Big Boss what country I come from. Ushi answers. There are a few people like me, a minority people, she says, living in the northwest of China, impoverished, uneducated. They try to hire a few of us to help us out. We send the money we earn back home to our families.

The men nod. I've long ago stopped blushing, and think only of rotten potatoes.

I drink my drugged tea when it's brought around instead of pouring it against the table leg to form a little puddle on the floor as I always do. I hope it will dull my brain. I don't want to think about my life right now.

There is whispered talk about the visitors as we stand in line for food at ten thirty, so tired our legs barely hold us up. If we had hopes that someone might find out what happens within these factory walls and help us, that fantasy has been crushed. No one will ever be allowed to talk. And if the visitors knew what was happening, would they really care?

I'm restless. I dream—only I am not asleep, so it is not a dream, but thoughts, memories that come to me in the blackness of night. I think of our farm. How we carefully fill irrigation ditches with precious water that brings life to our desert oasis, to our gardens and fruit trees. The apricots should be ready to harvest now, still firm, not yet too soft, just in between and perfect. Maybe there are a few early melons. I can almost see the field—Aygul and I are there picking the first ripe melon from the vine and eating it, the juice dripping down our faces as we chew slice after slice all the way to the rind.

I feel a pull on my arm. I'm sure it's Mother telling us we're much too old to make such a mess. Except that the pulling is not gentle but urgent.

I open my eyes and see Mikray. Her finger covers my mouth before words can come out. Then she cups my ear with her hands and whispers.

"I'll be gone for a few hours." She speaks quickly and softly—maybe I'm still asleep and dreaming. "I have to do it. Don't cover for me." Her voice catches. "If I can't make it back, I won't *come* back—ever. No one else must get in trouble." She reaches for my hand, squeezes it. "Thank you, Roshen, for being my friend." And she's gone.

There's no sound of footsteps as she leaves. I lean over the edge of my bed. Her bunk is empty. It's no dream—it's too real—and I'm scared. I don't want to be left alone. Mikray was sent to me by Allah to be my teacher and guide. I know that as I picture her stealing away into the darkness. So strong, with wisdom beyond her years.

Is she right to trust the person who is helping her? If she's caught, she could end up in one of the awful secret prisons and never be seen again. They might kill her and use her heart or kidneys or liver to make some Chinese official healthy. She must know all this. Such an ending is different from being sealed up in this disreputable factory that no one seems to care much about, even the government.

Make it back in time, Mikray! I say in silent prayer. *May Allah be with you.*

Will I ever be as brave as she is? Do more than stay locked within these walls, hearing the voices of jailed poets in my head, with no voice of my own?

Sixteen

THERE IS A rumor that we'll soon finish the blue coverall job, be paid, and get a day off. Hawa announces she'll speak to Ushi, or Big Boss, and insist they let us out of here. She leaves the factory floor the next day with a little boss. There's a smug look on her face when she returns.

This could be great news. If it's real. If Mikray leads us to a black café. If Mikray's friend who told her about the café has not already alerted the police to arrest us when we get there because we're underage. If the fake accounts Ahmat and I set up are still valid. The government changes rules from day to day, and I've been away from home for more than seven weeks.

At lunchtime I slip a note to Mikray. Grateful that she's still here. I've written *black café?* in small letters on a tiny piece of paper. One of us will end up eating it, so all our messages are short.

She steals a glance. Nods yes. She brings her hand to her mouth, chews for a few seconds, and swallows.

———

Ushi blocks our door at lunchtime to announce that tomorrow is a day off. "You may leave," she says, "but no one is to go out alone, and you must declare your plans before you can go." A special requirement for Uyghurs only. She says nothing about telling the truth.

I find it less unpleasant than usual to return to back-breaking, hand-wrecking work, knowing that at the end of the day we will have our turn with the paymaster, a good night's sleep, and a day off.

Finally the machines stop, and we line up in front of the humorless man who shows up now and then at Big Boss's side and is, apparently, our paymaster. He sits in front of a large ledger and piles of yuan notes. A self-protective instinct grips us Uyghurs, and we end up together at the back of the line. Each one of us has been caught speaking Uyghur, and we don't—yet—know how much each word will cost us.

Adile is the first to reach the pay table and give her name. The paymaster searches the ledger, then looks up. He leans back on his elbows and glares at all of us.

"Why are you here? You really think you can pay for your trip, the food you eat, your uniforms, in a few short weeks? Ha-ha-ha. Real funny," he says in a voice that has no laughter. "Dreamers, aren't you." He taps the ledger a few times with his finger. "Quite a few points here too, on some of you."

He slams the ledger shut. Picks up what's left of the yuan notes. And leaves.

We watch the money—our money, money we've labored endless, grueling hours for—being carried away.

I press my body against Mikray's to keep from tearing after him and wiping the look from his face, the look that lets us know we're the lowest of low people on earth. I want these people to know I despise them for what they're doing to us. I feel Mikray's body tremble, but she doesn't move. "Keep calm," she whispers. "He's only a little boss." We both stand immobile as we take in the new reality— that it may be many more weeks, months, before we're paid.

Why weren't we told we would have to pay back all these expenses before we came? I'd have come anyway. I would never have let Father lose the farm. But Zuwida and Jemile volunteered so they could send money to their families. We've worked past midnight and gotten up at five for the last week, and the two of them have talked of nothing but the extra money they were earning. Money they'd send home. A Chinese girl offered to take them to an honest place where someone would help them do this. Then they'd have lunch and tea together at the girl's favorite place. Maybe that can happen next time.

We walk up the stairs at a funereal pace. The promise of a special meal tonight to mark the completion of another great success for the Hubei Work Wear Company is of no interest.

I go to our room and pull my bag out from under the bunk, open the secret pocket, and count the money I have. Will it buy enough internet time for me to read Ahmat's messages and say everything I want to? With no knowledge of when we'll be paid, I must save some of my money in case we're allowed out again.

I yank the zipper closed. Shove the bag back under the bed and sit with my hands clasped in front of me. Upset that I didn't take all the money Father offered me. But I didn't need to take money from the family. I was to be a factory girl and earn my own.

The smell of food invades my nostrils. The garbage they make us pay for is being served. If I had money I'd go hungry now and eat all I want tomorrow, tons of delicious food. Maybe everyone in our room thinks that. There's no rush to line up. In time, we all go to the end of the food line.

I can't get rid of the anger that seethes inside me. I glance at the ceiling, at the moldings. We've never been sure whether or not the hallway is wired. I still see nothing, but there's no proof in that. I mumble to myself, then I can't hold back. "Why didn't we—why didn't *I* demand to see records?" I hiss loud and clear. It's much more than a whisper. "Aren't we at least owed an accounting of how much we've earned, how much we're still in debt? It's our right to know."

I've been heard. Those around me drop their heads or turn away. There's probably some device that's recorded my voice, maybe taken my picture. I'm not sure why I took the risk, but I had to.

It's Zuwida who comes to me. Takes my hand. "We have no rights, Roshen," she whispers. "No person, no laws on our side." I squeeze her hand. Once again numb and mute, and wondering if they'll ever pay us, I move slowly forward, led by the wise child who knows, as I do, that my stupid ranting will not change the way of things.

I hate that I'm standing here, holding out my bowl to accept the stingy ladle of soup they offer. There's more chicken than usual, actual chunks, most likely added so the girls who visit their families won't complain so much about the bad food. I give it the sniff test to make certain there's no pork or pork broth. It's okay. I won't have to throw it down the toilet.

No one talks as we sit on our bunks eating. No one wants to speak Mandarin, and it may cost us dearly to even whisper Uyghur.

My eyes are on Zuwida. When she's finished eating, I go to her. Take her bowl. "I'll wash it tonight," I say, leaning close to her ear, choosing still to speak Uyghur, whispering in my softest voice. Zuwida should not have to be burdened with Mandarin today. I stroke her hair, gently kiss her forehead. "Try to get a good night's sleep. Surely, in time, they'll pay us." I have no reason to believe this to be true, but someone has shown kindness to Zuwida. Maybe there will be more goodness coming to her.

She smiles. Then reaches beneath her bunk for the thermos that is always there and takes a few swallows.

When I return from washing our bowls, Zuwida is sleeping, either from exhaustion or from the tea that seems to help restore her body and bring her some kind of peace.

I have no tea, no thought of giving in to exhaustion or letting go of my anger. How can any of us do that? Hawa, for one, seems to be able to. She sits on the floor in front of her mirror, dabbing a brush into a small jar, painting her eyelids purple. Practicing her look for her big day. Nothing, I guess, can spoil her plans. She takes a pencil and outlines her eyes in black, until she looks like an ancient Egyptian, or one of the painted Chinese mannequins I've seen in the fancy stores in Hotan. I want to tell her to go wash her face. But how can I, a naïve country mouse, warn Hawa about the risk of walking around like that? Maybe only innocents like Jemile are treated badly, pawed and grabbed by ugly, lecherous men.

I wrap my arms around my body, wanting to erase all thoughts of treachery and think only of Ahmat. I try to remember the feeling of his arm against mine, comforting me, loving me. The thought that I might soon read a message from Ahmat electrifies my body with a heat that has nothing to do with weather.

This is something Ushi cannot take away from me.

Seventeen

MIKRAY AND I line up in front of the sign-out table. Gulnar joins us. I don't like it, but a sign from Mikray tells me she arranged it. I know nothing about Gulnar, except that she never talks and spends every free moment she has with her head bent over her stitchery. I don't want her going with us. Nothing must go wrong this morning. It's enough that I have to depend on Mikray.

Just get out of here, then deal with it, I tell myself.

"Well, look what we've got here." Ushi's voice erupts in laughter as she calls the group in front of us forward. "Going out on the town, are you, girls?" she says, surveying the quartet approaching her desk. Hawa and her entourage have joined up with a Chinese girl who has overnight acquired pink hair, eye shadow that extends from her cheeks to her eyebrows, and a huge, red splash of color over her lips. Hawa's face looks almost pale in comparison, but she matches the girl inch for inch in the shortness of her skirt, the high heels of her shoes, and the cleavage revealed by her sleeveless blouse.

"And where are you going, girls?" Ushi asks.

"A café and then an afternoon disco," the Chinese girl

answers, giving what she must think is a French accent to her Mandarin.

"Okay." Ushi draws out the word. "Sign right here. And remember the curfew." I'm surprised her voice loses some of its amusement as she says this, considering how much she enjoys giving out points.

Mikray, Gulnar, and I move forward, looking very Uyghur in our long skirts and leggings, blouses that cover our arms and breasts. We wear no makeup.

"Yes? Where are you going?" Ushi has her usual sour face as she looks back and forth between Mikray and me. She seems to take no interest in Gulnar, and that's probably in our favor.

"We're going to use the pitiful amount of money we have to buy some decent food, and then we hope to find a park, sit in the rain, and speak Uyghur," Mikray says in a voice loud enough for all to hear.

Everyone freezes, except Ushi. Her eyes twitch. Her mouth clamps over words I'm sure I've never heard before. I think she's going to explode if her face gets any redder. Then, worse. She starts to smile.

"Maybe," Ushi says, teeth showing, "I should go with you. I wouldn't want you all to get lost, or hurt walking around the neighborhood by yourselves. Lots of poor *Chinese* migrants live there, who might not like you on their streets."

She stops talking and sits with a fixed grin on her face. Staring at Mikray. Who stares back, a grin on her face too.

After a while Mikray shrugs. "Whatever," she says. "Can we leave now, or do we have to wait?"

Ushi turns red again as her jaw tightens. She thrusts her arm out, points to a spot along the wall. "You'll stand there until I'm ready."

Why, Mikray? Why did you do this to us! I scream silently as I force my legs to carry me the three meters to the side.

Mikray stands between Gulnar and me, her body rigid. "I'm sorry," Mikray whispers. "I hate her." She pauses. "I lost control." Her body shudders. I feel sorry for her. She has the courage to say what I let fester in my mind—I'm in awe of her for that—but I can't forgive her for jeopardizing our day off. How much longer must I go before I hear from Ahmat and let him know he's not forgotten? And that I love him?

I watch as Jemile, Zuwida, and Adile move forward. The Chinese girl is with them in spite of the fact that she will not need to lead them to a bank. There is no money to send home today. Ushi asks no questions, waves them on with barely a glance. I'm glad they're not wandering about alone.

Patime, Letipe, and Nurbiya stand in front of Ushi now. She looks at them as if she's never seen them before. "I can't imagine you'll cause much trouble. Go," she barks, her eyes already turning toward us.

Mikray, Gulnar, and I are now the only people in the room with Ushi. She motions for us to come before her.

No plan has been made. I'm surprised when Gulnar

steps in front of us. "It's raining so heavily now, I wonder if you could suggest something for us to do. Something that you would enjoy." Her voice is smooth, as soothing as her gentle face. "I'm sorry you have to give up your day off on our account, but we're grateful to you for the offer," she says.

Ushi, who looks as if she wants to bite our heads off, leans back in her chair and puts one hand on her waist while she holds her chin with her other hand.

"Yeah," she says. "Why don't you all go out and play in the rain. I'll let the neighborhood take care of you. I don't need to get wet." She pushes the book toward us. "Here, sign out."

It's raining hard when we go outside. No thunder, no lightning, just rain pelting our faces and forming puddles for us to wade through. We dodge across the busy highway into a warren of streets and alleys, wishing we had umbrellas, taking shelter under an overhang to catch our breath. There are many overhangs on this busy, narrow street and lots of people like us, without umbrellas, skittering from place to place trying to keep dry. But they're not really like us. The men are shirtless—bare-chested—and they wear short pants. Even the women wear shorts and scanty tops; old women have bare legs.

Litter and piles of garbage and construction debris line this half-paved street of two-story gray buildings. Children run around, enjoying the rain, which has to feel better to them than the scorching sun of a hot summer day. A car slowly honks its way through the narrow passage, zigzag-ging around people sitting under umbrellas in front of their shops, their tables full of wares. This is a street with no sidewalks, a street for people and bicycles and motorcycles, not cars.

We're about to make a dash to another dry spot when a hunched-over woman passes by, dragging a cart full of garbage by the shafts as if she were a donkey. No one seems to notice; some step out of their way to let her pass.

"We have to help her," I say.

"No." Mikray holds out her arm, stopping me. "It's not that we shouldn't," she says. "It's just that . . . we don't have time." She starts to move away.

I stop her. "Why, Mikray? Is it dangerous? Is that what Ushi meant when she said she'd let the neighborhood take care of us?"

"Oh no. These people are as poor and downtrodden by big bosses as we are. Maybe more. They won't hurt us. They think we're strange, wearing all these clothes when it's so hot," Mikray says. "Ushi probably meant she hopes I'll try to escape. Then she can have me tracked down and arrested and sent for reeducation. Please, for now we have to hurry."

Mikray's voice is sharp, urgent, as she bolts away, leading us on through more streets and alleys. She stops in front of a doorway covered with a green curtain that hangs from a rod on brass rings. A kid's lime-green cart is parked under an open window; an assortment of soggy kids' clothes droop from a line strung along the wall. No sign is visible. It's obviously someone's home, but Mikray parts the curtains and we walk into a tiny computer repair shop. A few old computers line rickety shelves. Others lie on tables, gutted with wires and parts hanging from them. Mikray greets a young man who is working on one of the machines—or, rather, gives him a nod. He stops what he's doing, opens a door at the back of his shop, and they disappear.

When they come back, Mikray collects money from us and tells us we each have a half hour. We don't have to sign papers or show registration cards. Nothing. We follow her through the door, then through another door, and enter a windowless room with about ten computers. Two people are already here and don't even look up to see who came in. With no discussion, we part and take seats that separate us. None of us has shared her secrets, and for now that is how it will be.

I touch the jade piece that hangs around my neck and pray that my connection to Ahmat works. Water trickles down my cheeks as I key in my password.

If it's rain, the raindrops turn to tears of joy. It works!

There are pages of messages. I start at the top and read as quickly as I can about the flow of water from the melting snows of the Kunlun Mountains. Our code words are simple so that we won't get caught in the great firewall the Chinese government has set up to censor communication in our Uyghur homeland of East Turkestan—a name we definitely will never use. Water is safe. If the streams bring an abundant supply, it means that all is well with Ahmat and with my family. If there has been a fierce windstorm from the desert, then there is trouble. I read on and on about streams that are full to overflowing, and about how Ahmat's job of conserving this precious resource has become harder and harder. He knows that this water must sustain him and the crops and the land for a long time to get past the period of drought that he knows will come. He, too, is counting the days, weeks, and months that we are separated.

I read on, and know he's getting desperate for news. *A thousand years are not worth one day,* he writes. Just that sentence from the famous sung poetry of our people, and I know I am to fill in the words:

> *Without love my soul*
> *A thousand years are not worth one day.*
> *Before the fires of love*
> *The fires of hell are nothing.*
> *You bring me terrible pain.*

I rest my hands on the keyboard and close my eyes as I think these lines, struggling to find the right words for my reply.

It's when I open my eyes that I sense a change. Movement. A shadow crosses my screen. A man has passed by.

Was he standing behind me, reading my screen, while my eyes were closed? I steal a glance at Mikray and see that she's cleared her screen and sits hunched over the keyboard as if in deep concentration. The man passes her by too and goes over to a man who was already in the café when we entered, obviously taking him by surprise. The video on the man's screen keeps rolling until the intruder reaches over, ejects the disk, and puts it in his satchel. It's easy to tell that the jerk of his head means *Come with me.* They leave very quickly.

Were they friends? Was the video watcher being arrested?

There's no way of knowing. We seem to be safe. It wasn't underage people he was looking for—or Uyghurs. No informer alerted him to strangely dressed girls running in the rain.

My hands are shaking. I'm not certain I can type, but I must send a message to Ahmat before time is up.

I key, *The sky is gray. The moon is good, the sun is good . . .* Ahmat will know the rest of the words, or he'll find them. I can think of no other safe words to send that will let him know how I am and why I haven't answered sooner.

I turn to his emails again, wanting to read every one. Each is shorter than the one before. Sometimes he sends only the word "water." Twice he's written "wind" with a string of question marks following it. I keep searching for words to let him know I might not have another chance to send a message for weeks or months, without alarming him so much that he will get in trouble trying to find me.

A tap on my shoulder startles me. It's Mikray. I can't go yet! I can't break the connection. I've written so little.

Mikray tugs at me. "Roshen," she says, "we must leave."

I sign off and follow Mikray and Gulnar through the doors and into the street, thinking of what I should have said. Why did I send so few words? I could have said, *Work, work, work, so little time.* Those are safe words and would have given him some understanding of my life. His words comforted me. The words I've sent to him—when he finds the poem—speak only of my despair:

I am far from my homeland and the sky is gray.
The moon is good, the sun is good, to be a wanderer is bad.
I am a wanderer, the prince of wanderers.
I cannot bear this wandering, my face is sallow.

Eighteen

MIKRAY LEADS US to a small teahouse. Gulnar and I don't ask how she knows about it, we simply follow. We decided before we came that we'd have tea. No food —we couldn't afford that—but we would have tea. We sit at a table near the front window. Mikray makes sure that Gulnar sits with her back to the street. She herself sits so that she can look out. I have a partial view of life as it is lived on this gray street in the drizzle of rain falling from the gray sky.

As if by agreement, each of us takes a headscarf from her bag. Gulnar and I tie ours loosely at the back. Mikray pulls hers tightly across her brow.

The tea is so good. Steamy hot in a bowl. It isn't the steamy hot I need in this sweltering weather, it's the comfort of my hands cupping the bowl, taking small sips to make it last.

We don't say much. My mind is on the messages I should have sent to Ahmat. I didn't tell him how much his weather reports mean to me, or that he should keep sending as many as he can, even though I have no way of knowing when I'll be able to reply.

"I'm going for a walk. Alone," Mikray says, bringing

me back from the anguish of my thoughts. "I'll be a while. If you want, there's a space nearby where you can sit outdoors under a scraggly tree and electric wires. Ask the owner. He'll tell you how to get there." She gets up slowly, as if she's not in a rush, and I know why. She doesn't want Gulnar to know she's meeting the young man who's sitting on his motorcycle at the corner of the street—the young man from the factory. His name is Chen. Is he a friend or a traitor?

"We'll be fine, Mikray." I put my hand over hers as she pushes away from the table. "Thank you for helping us." I'm fighting to hold back tears of gratitude and of concern for her.

Her eyes meet mine. "Wait for me at the park," she says, and somewhere buried in the permanent scowl that covers her face is that flicker of defiance that unnerves me and at the same time makes me care for her.

"Off you go," I say, and I don't let my eyes follow her.

I turn to Gulnar. "I'm quite content to sit here for a while. How about you?" I say this so that she'll look at me, not Mikray. Then I find myself talking about Ahmat, at first to distract her and then because I need to tell someone. I tell her how he seems so far away, so unreal to me.

"No," Gulnar says. "You're the lucky one. You mustn't lose faith. He cares for you. How many messages did he send?" Her face, always so tranquil, so at peace, comes alive. "You're so lucky," she says again, and then her face crumples.

"Was there bad news, Gulnar?" I ask.

Her hands cover her face. She shakes her head.

Whatever is wrong, I know she has not been comforted by our visit behind the green curtain.

"Can you tell me what's happened? Can I help?" I say. I pour what is left in our teapot into her bowl and put it into her hands, which have fallen onto the table. Something familiar, something comforting may help.

"Thank you," she whispers as she wraps her fingers around the bowl.

"I was about to be married," she finally says, her voice quiet, almost under control. "But they took my fiancé away. It was a peaceful protest—it started out peacefully." I'm afraid she'll break the tea bowl as her hands tighten in an iron grip. After a pause, she leans nearer to me. "They fired guns at him. At the Uyghurs. He fought back. . . . He was captured and sent off . . . somewhere . . . to prison. I signed up to work in the factory because I need money. I need it to help find him, maybe bribe someone to tell me where he is." Her face tightens in anger. "Even if I have money, I'm not sure I'll ever find out if he's dead or alive. There are no traces, no news or rumors from anyone at home." She pushes her chair away from the table. Stands up. "Let's go outside," she says. "It's stopped raining." I stay motionless. *Ahmat is always careful, isn't he? He hates what is happening, but . . . ? Is he still cautious and wise?* I must be like Gulnar, who hides her feelings in her embroidery, carefully, methodically adding stitches to her ever-larger tapestry of colorful desert tamarisk. Work that belies her despair.

It's Ahmat from whom I must conceal the truth, so he knows nothing of what's happening here. He must not try to help me. He must think only of his studies and my return. Harbor no more anger than he already has for the tyrants who rule over us. Saying nothing is how I can help to keep Ahmat and my family safe. I pray that he will not read too much truth in my words, that he'll think I said *I cannot bear this wandering* because I'm so far away from him and all I hold dear.

I get directions from the teashop owner. Gulnar and I walk slowly and silently through streets that have become more crowded with half-dressed people and pushcarts and wares, children splashing and climbing over piles of debris—everyone dodging bicycles and motorbikes as they speed by.

When we get to the park, we find overturned wooden crates to sit on. Mikray was right—there is a sad-looking, almost leafless tree, and there are electrical wires dangling above the small grassless space.

"I wish it were still raining," I say to Gulnar. "I prefer hot rain to the steam bath we're sitting in now."

She nods, and for a while we speak about the weather. Then about Hawa and her entourage. They left the factory with umbrellas, which was curious. No one in Hotan owns, or needs, an umbrella.

"The girl with the pink hair must have provided them," I say.

"No. Ushi gave them the umbrellas. I saw her do it." Gulnar shrugs.

I hope Hawa will be all right in the hands of the pink-haired one. It's certain she's being taken to a place much different from where we are.

"I guess it's Zuwida and Jemile I really worry about," I say, "but the Chinese girl they're with seems kind. I hope she'll at least buy them tea."

"I hope so," Gulnar says. She sighs and turns her head away. Not rudely, but I think she is lost in her own thoughts, while I'm doing all I can to avoid mine.

I let the sounds of the neighborhood take over. Familiar noises—children laughing and crying, neighbors calling to one another, motorcycles honking their way through crowded streets. But they aren't the sounds of my people. I shut my eyes as if doing so will make it all go away, and in a way it does. My eyelids are heavy. I can't keep them open. My head rests against the pitiful tree.

I don't know how much time passes before I wake up. Gulnar paces back and forth across the small square of parched earth, kicking at the trash that's been dumped there. It's comforting to know she has watched over me. When she sees I'm awake, she sits beside me.

Our stomachs growl.

"At home," I say, "my family is known to have the

sweetest, juiciest watermelons at market. You must visit one day—when we return. We'll feast on watermelon." I lick my dry, cracked lips, hoping the thought might help quench my thirst. "I have dreams about our melon patch."

"That's a good dream," Gulnar says, but she is not thinking of eating or of home. She keeps looking up at the sky, and now I look up too. That's the way we tell time, and time is passing too quickly.

"Mikray will be here." Now I get up and start walking back and forth. I know what I say is the truth—unless something bad happens. "She won't abandon us."

It's not long, though, before smells of cooking oil and spices mix with the hot, humid air and mothers call children in for supper. It becomes harder to know the time because the sky is threatening again. A black cloud heads our way.

I listen for sounds of motorcycles coming from the alleys that feed into the park or from the narrow street. Many pass. None of the passengers is Mikray.

"Do you know the way back to the factory?" Gulnar asks. "I wasn't paying much attention."

I think of the alleys and the turns we made to get to the black café, and the answer is no. I shake my head. "You wait here," I say. "I'm going to the teahouse to get directions."

I'm gone before she can stop me, before I can respond to the panic on her face.

The directions are vague, and I'm told two different

routes. We probably should leave now, before the rain starts again, but we can't. At least I can't. Maybe that is what Ushi meant when she said she'd let the neighborhood take care of us. She thought—hoped—Mikray would get in trouble and never return.

There are men sitting on our overturned boxes when I get back, playing a game on a wooden board they've put between them. Other men hang around, smoking, talking. Home from work. Relaxing before supper.

Gulnar crouches in the shadow of a building next to the park. I join her.

"It's getting late," Gulnar says, her voice strained, unnatural. "We don't know our way, and the men . . . I don't like it."

"Gulnar, please. The men don't seem to be taking any notice of us. Pull off your scarf," I tell her as I quickly remove mine. "Keep hunched over. With our rained-on, bedraggled clothes, we don't look much different from the woman we saw earlier pulling the cart. Mikray will be here," I say. "She gave her word. She'll come. We still have time."

Gulnar shakes her head. Keeps shaking it.

"If we're late, I'll tell Ushi it's my fault and she can give me your points."

Gulnar drops her head when she hears my words and the unkindness in my voice, but I can't help it. She chose to come with us, to go to a black café. Surely she had some idea of the risks.

I turn away. My eyes search for Mikray; my mind tries to will her back. I'd never admit to Gulnar that I, too, am losing hope for her return. I have faith in Mikray, but I don't trust the young man from the factory. Is he Ushi's secret agent, getting Mikray into trouble so she can be sent away?

Mikray doesn't come, only debris stirred up by gusts of wind, and then the rain—heavy, almost horizontal rain—begins to soak us. The men leave the park. Gulnar and I flatten ourselves against the side of the building, getting as much protection as possible from the narrow overhang.

The rain brings something else—an umbrella sweeping down the alley. Then I see leggings, a long skirt.

"Mikray, here!" I shout, waving my arms.

She greets us. Presses herself against the wall next to us. She doesn't tell us where she's been. I look for some sign that her venture has met with success, but her face holds its hard, angry expression.

"I brought you something," Mikray says. She turns to me, thrusts the umbrella into my hands. "Hold this." She runs into the park and drags the crates over to the wall. We sit, crowding together under the umbrella. She pulls plastic bags from her pocket, opens one, and takes out a handful of dates for each of us, dropping them into our palms. They're beautiful, large red dates—the kind grown in Hotan.

Only when I find myself stuffing my mouth with the smooth, juicy flesh of the dates do I realize how hungry I was. I savor the sweetness, the familiar taste. Suck on the small pits to get every last bit of flesh from them before spitting them out and putting more dates into my mouth.

When I finally stop gorging, I look around to see Mikray spitting out pits, licking her lips. She must have been as hungry as we were. Gulnar still has uneaten dates in her hand. She is eating them politely, one at a time. Our eyes meet; we all burst into laughter. A giddy, silly sound, and I marvel that we can still find such joy in a mouthful of dates.

We ignore the time and the weather and celebrate with a small ceremony. The rain pelts down on us as we shove the pits over to the barren park and bury them in soft mud. "May the good people of this town someday—a few years from now—enjoy the dates they pick from the trees that will grow from the seeds we plant here today," I say.

"There's more," Mikray announces when we're back huddled against the building. She opens a second bag and hands each of us a few walnuts. Hotan dates, and now Hotan walnuts! How has she made this happen?

For a moment a vision of home flashes before me. I'm shuffling through fallen leaves on the lane beside the farm, picking up walnuts, sitting under the tree to eat them.

"For our pockets," Mikray says. "Let's get out of here. Now. Run."

My vision disappears, and under the cover of one flimsy umbrella we dash through monsoon winds and rain into a maze of winding, narrow streets that lead back to our prison.

Nineteen

FOR TWO WEEKS we've been cutting through bolts of heavy brown cotton duck—"fire resistant, for welding," we've been told. It's hard to cut. Production has slowed. Only half the sewing machines still work. Big Boss bought cheap machines that can't handle the job, but he has ordered new ones. Until the new machines are brought in, sewing will be done in two twelve-hour shifts. No lunch or dinner break, but the next twelve hours to eat and sleep and recover. Cutting hours are divided into four six-hour shifts. We alternate shifts so our paralyzed hands have a chance to uncramp. Girls in finishing do twelve-hour shifts. Their ironing and packing job is easiest, so they're expected to fill in when people keel over from exhaustion.

There's one good side to this order. September has become unseasonably warm. If it becomes so hot that the factory spontaneously bursts into flame, I can cover myself with fire-resistant material and try to escape. Also, by simple math, working twelve hours a day is better than working fifteen or sixteen or more, especially when you have no idea if you'll ever be paid.

It's midafternoon when Ushi walks through, for once not paying much attention to us or lashing out at our laziness. She returns quickly, followed by Hawa. Hawa doesn't seem distressed. In fact, she has a haughty look on her face as she walks down the aisle in her tall, elegant way. Finishing obviously doesn't exact the same toll as cutting or sewing. She and Ushi disappear through the door, and I presume it's not the toilet they're going to. Hawa must be going on a special visit to the executive quarters.

A while later Ushi returns—alone—and goes to the pink-haired girl, whose hair today is back to its normal pale purple. The girl works in cutting, but she stands too far away for me to overhear what is said. They leave too.

I keep watching the door. None of them return.

Nadia, the other Uyghur member of my cutting-crew shift, keeps looking at the door and then at me. I think she knows something about what's happening and is bursting to tell. As the third member of the Hawa-Rayida trio, her role seems to be offering constant flattery and admiration to the other two. She's the student of their self-importance.

My shift ends at six o'clock, and because they no longer bother to collect scissors, I drop mine midcut and rush to the bottom of the stairs, where Jemile will be waiting for me. It's become our habit to meet for a quick hug and a few words as I leave my six-hour scissor shift and she begins hers. That means she has to wait for one of the Uyghur sewers or finishers to sign out for the toilet before she dares to go, but it has worked out.

The stairs are clear now that the shifts have changed, except for Nadia, waiting for me. The stairs are a good place to talk. We haven't found any electronic devices there, and with the different schedules, there are fewer people on the stairs at any one time.

"Do you know what's happening with Hawa?" I ask in Uyghur, keeping my voice low.

"No. Not really," Nadia says, and lets her face collapse. What I thought was eagerness to tell was apparently anxiety. "She said she had some kind of special arrangement, but I don't know what it is. Do you think she's all right?"

"I hope so, Nadia. She appears quite able to take care of herself."

We're totally alone on the stairs. I risk another few minutes, although we've become paranoid about being discovered; little bosses sometimes monitor shift changes. I whisper another question. "The Chinese girl who was with you on your day off—why did Ushi take her from the room too? What do you know about her?"

"Her name is Quin Fong. She's from a city near here. Knows a lot of places to go, like the right shops for clothes and the kind of shoes we all like. She's nice," Nadia says, flipping her hair around in that awkward way she has when she tries to imitate Rayida.

"Yeah. Good," I say as I turn and make my way up the stairs.

"Ushi arranged for her to go with us. We had a fun day," Nadia says, trailing my steps.

"Oh?" I stop. "Ushi arranged it?" I look at Nadia, who still has a *had a fun day* expression on her face. She nods, still happy. Oblivious. Ushi arranged for their "fun day," gave them umbrellas so they wouldn't get wet. She does nothing out of kindness. What does she want from them? From Hawa?

"Let's go eat," I say. "I'm hungry and tired." I don't tell her there's a hollow feeling inside me. Something more than fun is happening. I'm certain it's Big Boss, not Ushi, who has a special interest in Hawa.

There's a lot of activity on the sleeping floor as girls get ready for the seven o'clock night shift and those just released line up for the toilet and then for food.

I get my food and sit on Mikray's bunk to eat, wishing she were here. With different working shifts we have little awake time together.

In our room it's quieter than usual. The mystery of Hawa's exit has been talked out; there are now only stolen glances at Nadia sitting alone on Hawa's bunk. Many shrugged shoulders.

When we have finished eating, Nadia and I go together to wash our bowls, fill them with hot water, and bring them back to the room. We've learned that it helps to soak our hands for a few minutes and then massage them. Our fingers will be less stiff when we go down at midnight for our next shift.

I'm methodically rubbing my palm when there's an eruption of squeals and Mandarin jabber in the hallway. This kind of outburst is usually caused by something trivial, such as a change of hair color. I pay little attention until the noise travels to our door and Hawa walks in. Actually, I think her intent was to sweep in, but her entrance doesn't quite have that kind of flair. Nor does she make eye contact with anyone.

Shopping bags dangle from her arms. She's wearing an outfit I've never seen before. A filmy loose top with a wide, low neck and puffy short sleeves falls nearly to the bottom of her short black skirt, which barely covers her. It definitely shows off her beautiful long legs and the strappy black shoes with ridiculous high heels she's teetering on.

She goes to her bunk and deposits her packages next to Nadia, who sits there holding her bowl of hot water, gaping.

"What's happening, Hawa?" Nadia whines. "I was so worried."

"No reason to be," Hawa says, reaching under her bunk and pulling out her bag. She begins gathering her few belongings and throwing them in. "It's what was agreed upon when my father signed me up. He wouldn't have let me come without the prospect of a job that would help build my career." She doesn't look at Nadia when she says this, busily untying the mirror she had attached to a rail. "I'm finally getting what was promised. I'm to help Boss Lee." She unwinds the scarf she used to decorate the bunk post and throws it into her bag.

"Come on, Kitten," a voice says from the door. It's the Chinese girl with the pale purple hair. "They're waiting for us downstairs."

My eyes follow every move of "Kitten" as she turns to leave our room, weighed down with her packages and traveling bag. The pale purple–haired Chinese girl, Quin Fong, does not move to help her, and perhaps the rest of us in the room are too stunned to think to offer—or there is something in her bearing that tells us to leave her alone. Not arrogance exactly. More like determination. Fierce determination.

For an instant she lets our eyes meet, and I see a look that stings my heart. "Hawa!" I cry. I reach out to her.

She throws her head back with a shake that means *stay away* and passes into the hallway.

Twenty

I LEAN AGAINST the rails of my bed, bewildered by what just happened. I know now that Hawa is scared to death. It might have been easy for her to change from Hawargul to Hawa, but the change from Hawa to Kitten might not be her choice. Uyghur girls are not called Kitten; Chinese girls are.

I crawl to my upper bunk, trying to get as far away from Nadia's wails as possible. I have no comfort to offer her. I tell myself I must sleep to be ready for the midnight shift, but sleep won't come. Maybe Hawa is right, and very brave, and really will be trained and learn skills that will help her to run a business when she gets back home. I'm resigned to letting a year of my life go unlived while my brain becomes soft, my skills rusty.

I'm the coward. Letting them win. I write my poet's poems in my notebook and ignore what they say. *Hey, poor Uyghur, wake up, you have slept long enough. You have nothing. What is now at stake is your very life.* The message is clear. Nothing can be gained by wallowing in self-pity.

And when I wake up—when I'm alive again—what will I do? I don't want to be called Kitten.

I have no time to think about my question. The seven

o'clock shift bursts into the room. They learned about Hawa on the stairway as the shifts changed places.

"Are you sleeping?" Mikray asks, even though she's looking right at me sitting on my bunk with my eyes open.

"Probably not," I say, and can't help but smile at the absurdity of everything.

"I didn't like her, but I don't think it's a good thing that just happened. I'm going for food. Come down when I get back," she says, and leaves.

I'm an observer now. Nadia and Rayida weep and flail around like lost lambs. I notice that Rayida has already claimed Hawa's bunk, which is closer to the window, and tied her scarf around the post.

I'm on Mikray's bunk when she returns. I've brought my pen and notebook and keep writing while she eats and washes her bowl. When she's beside me again, I pass my notebook to her. "Do you know who wrote this line?"

"Yes, I do," she says. "I know the next line too." She grabs the pen and writes, *Cut off the head of your enemy, spill his blood!* She uses my pen as if it's the handle of the rivet machine, pounding big black letters into the paper.

I take back my notebook and the pen—which I'm lucky she hasn't broken—and rip the page out. "You have to eat this one," I say, handing it to her.

Mikray crumples the paper and stuffs it into her mouth, chewing as if she were savoring the sweetness of a Hotan date.

She reaches under her sheet for her pad and pencil, but

I write another note and pass it to her before she can write anything. *You can't sneak out again. It's too dangerous. With the factory going day and night there's no good time.* I write in tiny letters. I'll eat this one.

She reads it. I pull my notebook back, rip off the corner where I've written, and stuff the paper into my mouth. Mikray holds her pencil, but she doesn't write. I think I've guessed right about what she was going to say.

Mikray curls her feet under her, leans back. "When do you think we might get back to our old schedule?" she asks.

"There are bolts and bolts of the heavy stuff stacked against the wall for us to cut. Maybe another two weeks, unless Big Boss gets the new machines. Even then, I don't think we can cut any faster, but I'm sure he'll make us try."

I lean closer. "There's talk on the stairs about finding new jobs. The girls don't think any money is going to be made on this order. Many are ready to leave. What have you heard?"

Mikray drops her head for a moment, then picks up her pad. *Chen is ready to quit. They're working him around the clock*, she writes. *Big Boss is a madman.* She rips off her note and stuffs it in her pocket. A treat for later.

Be wise, Mikray. Be cautious. Someone is always in the hallways. I show her what I've written. She arches her eyebrows. "Wise." "Cautious." These are words she does not know. Will I forget them too if I ever "wake up"?

———

I've been sleepless for at least nineteen hours. No way could anyone in our room sleep. Now it's midnight and here I am, cutting, cutting, cutting until there's no connection left between my body and my hand. I'm muttering —sleep-deprived grousing with every curse word I know in Uyghur and was never allowed to use.

Hey, Big Boss. Tell Hawa to bring me some energy tea. I'd like to shout the words, but I don't. *Where's my drug?* I'd drink it this morning—at least I think it's almost morning. It has to be.

I give myself little goals. *Five more pockets.* I can still count, I just can't keep my eyelids open long enough to see what I'm counting. My Chinese fellow cutters have solved this. They pinch their eyelids with clothespins to keep them open. Maybe I could borrow some cute little blue plastic clothespins from the seven-to-seven shifters. They're getting so much sleep now, they don't need them. Only the cutters are still sleep-deprived.

I'm drifting, but somehow the *clip-clop* of shoes getting closer and closer breaks through to my consciousness. Little Boss has spotted me and is on her way. She's a different little boss than usual—very large and very mean. She pokes us with a rod when she catches us slipping into dreamland. It's effective. I wake up enough to get my hand moving just by hearing her coming. No quick *crrrunch*, release to my scissors, more like *grrrrrunt*, pry the scissor blades apart and push down again, but I'm working. Counting. She stands behind me for a while, then spots someone else and moves on.

At six o'clock I crawl up the stairs, climb to my bunk, and collapse. Clothes still on. No breakfast. Only sleep is of interest. A few hours of oblivion.

"Have a good sleep, Roshen," I hear Mikray say with a gentleness in her voice that soothes my way into nothingness.

———

"Okay, everyone. Out! Off your beds. Into the hallway. I've been told you have things here I might be interested in knowing about. So I'm doing a little inspection." It's Ushi's voice. I turn over, see her standing in the middle of our room, shouting. Have I missed my shift? I blink to clear my eyes, look at the clock. It's only ten.

"Come on. Out. Don't bring anything with you." Ushi's not alone. One of the kitchen help is with her, also Chen, who stands there holding a cardboard box. His slumped body suggests he'd rather not be here, and I think better of him for that. He does us the favor of looking at the floor.

Except for me, who fell asleep with my clothes on, the girls who aren't downstairs working are scantily dressed. They pick up whatever they can find to cover themselves. "Oh no," Ushi says, grabbing a towel from Nadia and throwing it back on her bunk. "Do you think your bodies are so special we can't look at them? You're no different from the rest of us. Get going."

We follow Ushi's orders and file out the door. I stand as wide and protective as I can with the girls huddled behind me. The Chinese girls gather in the hallway to see what Ushi's hollering about, either giggling or sneering. They all but shout, *Disrobed Uyghurs on display.*

"Have we done something bad?" someone whispers. "Ushi never checks our room."

No one answers. I have no answer.

We hear Ushi barking orders through the closed door. "Open the bags," she says, and then we hear thuds, things being thrown around.

Ushi laughs. "Let's take their scarves. They're not going to need them for a long time. Punishment for thinking they deserve special treatment." She laughs some more, but she laughs alone.

After what seems an eternity, Ushi leads the procession out of our room. Passes us as if we didn't exist. The kitchen woman follows, carrying the box, which is heaped high with our belongings. Mikray's friend has Zuwida's mattress slung over his shoulder, her pillow clutched in his hand.

We move back into our room. I want to sit on Mikray's bed and cry, but I don't. Our bags have been turned upside down, the contents spilled onto the floor. I quickly grab Mikray's and my things and stuff them back into the bags before they're trampled on. I don't take inventory, but my scarf is gone. Ushi was careful to see to that.

I sit, watching the others collect their things, some taking time to be neat. Rayida is fingering the empty post where she had wrapped her scarf.

I try not to think about my notebook. I don't keep it in my bag, but it was barely hidden. There's a chance they might have overlooked it. As I stand to check, a horrible thought comes to me. My necklace. I don't feel it. I don't remember taking it off, but I've been so sleepy. Slowly I let my hand creep up my body until my fingers touch it. I gasp as I clutch the jade. It's sacred to me. My only connection to Ahmat.

When my heart stops pounding, I pull back the sheet that covers my plywood bed. My notebook is gone, and my pen. My notebook, which I was slowly filling with the poems of my poets and my own attempts to turn my feelings of loneliness for Ahmat and my family into poetry, taken from me. Gone, except for the poems I keep in my head and heart. How long will I remember the words I've written—the words I've cut, stitched, and ironed into my memory?

I hope Ushi will never know their meaning.

I check Mikray's space for her pad and pencil. They're both there, hidden alongside her orange and blue flowered scarf, which is neatly folded. I smile. Chen would know it was hers. We wore our scarves on our day off, when she was with him. I gain respect and trust for him, some of my faith in human kindness restored.

But there is an enemy among us. Someone who knew that Zuwida had a mattress and pillow. Someone who could gain favor by reporting this special treatment. Would Hawa so quickly betray Zuwida? She knew everything about the mattress and the teas. Hawa could easily have reported that someone was helping her. Is that why they raided the room? To punish us for this act of kindness shown to an undesirable?

Hawa has seen me write in my notebook many times. Did she tell them they might get good information by taking that, too? They wouldn't be able to read the Uyghur, but Hawa can. Will she decide how many points I get for all those Uyghur words? Then read Ushi the words of treason I've written down so they can send me away for reeducation?

Is Hawa the traitor? Would she do that?

I can't forget the look on her face as she left our room.

Twenty-One

I HAVE LITTLE MEMORY of working from noon until six o'clock. I did see Zuwida. She came to the exit door to sign out for the toilet. She was calm. She obviously knew nothing of what had happened upstairs earlier. Nadia and I were the only Uyghur girls who knew, and neither of us made a move to follow her and tell her. It was not a message to be recorded. The Chinese girls in cutting who knew about the raid would have no idea it was Zuwida's mattress and pillow that were removed. Even if they did, they wouldn't waste a toilet break to tell her.

I'm glum when I walk into our room after my shift. I hate the way they've separated us with different times for working and sleeping and eating. Today seems worse than ever. We need one another. We need to be together.

It isn't a good night. Cook doesn't have the food ready. Those going to work at seven holler at her. For the first time ever, Chen is in the kitchen helping—looking unhappy and out of place there, too. I stand-sleep in line, finally get food, eat as much as I can of the garbage, and curl up on Mikray's bunk to wait. Zuwida will be told what happened as she passes the girls going down to work the night shift. A few of us will be waiting for her in the room.

The wisp that is our Zuwida stands in the doorway, looking stronger than when we met her, but still fragile. Her lips, which have learned to laugh, hang limp and trembling. Her big black eyes—no longer sunk into her face—are open and alive, and filled with confusion. She goes to her bunk, falls to her knees, and crawls under the bed, her arms, hands, sweeping the floor.

She crawls back out. Her hands still. "It's gone," she whispers.

Adile's arms enfold her. "The thermos?"

Zuwida nods.

"Who does this for you? Who's helping you? Please tell me," Adile pleads. "I'll find them. We'll work out a new, secret way."

Zuwida pinches her lips together as she violently shakes her head no.

"Okay," Adile says. "If you won't tell, we'll go for food while they're still serving. You will eat and stay healthy."

It seems unlikely Zuwida will even make it off the floor, much less to the food line, but I go to her other side, and together Adile and I lift her up. Someone hands her a bowl and off we go. A hush surrounds us as we stand in line, maybe something like pity flowing from our Chinese coworkers.

"Don't make me do this," Zuwida pleads. "Let me go back. Please. I can't be here." She struggles to pull away with more strength than I expect, but Nurse Adile insists she eat, and the rules won't allow us to fill a bowl and take it to her.

I force Zuwida's arm toward the cook who is ladling the slops.

Cook thrusts the ladle toward her. Then halts. "You," she sneers. "You're the helpless urchin who disrupted my kitchen. I hope you choke on this." She splashes the food into Zuwida's bowl, which I'm holding in one hand while the other holds Zuwida up — until she slips away and runs to our room.

She's squeezed into a little ball of flesh in the corner of her plywood bunk by the time any of us catch up with her. "Was she there? Was she?" she moans.

"Who, Zuwida? Was who there?" Adile lays a firm hand on her shoulder.

"The other cook," she whispers. "She's the one who helps me. Her teas . . . they strengthen my lungs . . . help me breathe. She gave me extra food." Zuwida hides her face with her hands as she seems to sink further into her plywood bed. "She was afraid she'd get caught . . . with so many around." Her big eyes, no longer confused but frightened, peep through her fingers. "Was she there?"

The answer, of course, is no. Now I know why Mikray's friend was called in. Why our food was late, the kitchen in disarray. One of the cooks cared for Zuwida when we first came and she was ill and alone in the room. The teas in the thermos under the bed were the medicines that saved her life.

That will be no more. There's little doubt that the other cook has been fired.

"Who is the traitor?" I ask Mikray when I go back to our bunk. She sits quietly, stroking her scarf, which she has discovered carefully hidden under the sheet.

"Hawa, I suppose. That seems almost too obvious." She pauses, glances around the room. "It's getting dangerous here," she says in a voice I can hardly hear.

I look at her. I'm not sure of her meaning, of what she knows.

Meet me at the top of the stairs in a few minutes, she writes. She picks up her empty food bowl and heads toward the toilet. After a while I leave too. When the hallway is empty, I go through the stairway door and find her standing against the wall, in a shadow.

"I'm going to be leaving," Mikray says. "I don't know when, but I will be. Soon, I think."

I want to shout no. I can't think of being here without her. I force myself to stay calm.

"My father was a merchant and part of the resistance against communist rule. He wanted Uyghurs to have a voice in their own governance." Our heads are so close, I feel her spit on my face when she speaks. "He wouldn't let the police into our house without a permit . . . and now he's gone. Everything's gone. Forever. My brother escaped. My mother went into hiding. I tried to keep our business going, but the government forced me to come here."

Mikray's hand squeezes my arm. The quieter her voice,

the more urgently she grasps my arm. "The man who sells dates is Uyghur, from Hotan." Mikray pulls her face away. Her eyes meet mine. "You must meet him. Know who he is. He's a good man."

Our eyes hold for a moment as I nod. If any softness comes over her face, it's quickly replaced by her fierceness as she leans in again. "His suppliers in Hotan have found my mother. She has news from my brother. He escaped to Uzbekistan and wants us to join him. My mother has safe passage. I don't. And I'm being watched. I know it. There's a traitor here—more dangerous than Hawa, only I don't know who it is."

"But if you escape and are caught—you've heard the stories, Mikray. We all have. They'll kill you. Cut your organs out while you're still alive so they can sell them. They do horrible things."

"Wake up, Roshen. Wake up! I won't sit here and let them spill my blood. They've taken my father. It's my turn to spill their blood, somehow, from somewhere. Not from inside this factory."

Mikray's voice is too loud. I press my hand over hers. Still her for a moment.

"Just know this," she says more calmly. "You will find my bed empty. Do nothing. I may return. But then—someday—I'll be gone. You are to have no knowledge of this, of me, of my family, of my plans. They may try to force you, but stay innocent of anything to do with me, no matter what they do."

Now our hands pile up, one on top of the other as we cling together.

"I love you, Roshen. I wish we might have been friends in a different world."

She tries to pull her hands away, but I can't release her.

"You must let me go. I'm not good for our people here. It's you they need. And maybe, someday . . ." She pauses. Her forehead tightens as her eyes bore into mine. "Maybe you'll turn our stories into poems for the world to know."

And then she's gone. I wait a few minutes and peek into the hallway. When it's clear, I go to our room, crawl to my bunk, and hope for sleep.

Twenty-Two

STRAIGHTEN YOUR PILES," Little Boss scolds, her probe stick tapping the floor, the worktables, us. Anything in her path. "At least try to look alive," she says as she stops in front of one of the Chinese girls and holds out her hand. The girl removes the clothespins that hold her eyes open and hands them over. Little Boss goes around collecting clothespins. Something important must be happening today. Usually she tolerates things that help us work.

I've been in dreamland, which is seldom a pleasant place to be. Mikray is always leaving—speeding away on a motorcycle. I run to catch up with her, but I can't. I keep trying, trudging through floodwaters that get deeper and deeper, trying to follow, trying to reach her, but I never make it.

Stay awake, Roshen, I tell myself. At least I'm conscious enough to know that I'm still here, and so is Mikray. We still work in our shifts around the clock. Three weeks have passed and she hasn't snuck out. I'm grateful for that, even though I know her being here is not necessarily a good sign for her. We don't speak about it.

A rod hits my shoulder. "You're working slower than a snail," Little Boss says. "We're not paying you to sleep on the job."

A strangled sound escapes my lips. It could be a laugh. Doesn't she know what a fool she is? If you're being paid, you actually get money.

She hits me again. She knows it was a laugh.

"I'm awake," I say. "Thank you for hitting me to remind me of my duty."

She humphs and walks away, apparently not caring that I delivered these words in the most disrespectful voice I could find.

I watch Zuwida go up to the toilet sign-out. She's apparently told she can't leave. She heads back, a distressed but brave look on her face. Zuwida seems to be doing all right. I wonder if she might be the one person who is better off at the factory than she was at home. Here she's surrounded and cared for by so many. Hopefully the healing teas she was given have restored her body and will help carry her through. Cook treats her badly, but I have more than once seen Adile switch bowls with her when they get back to the room. Zuwida sleeps away most of her twelve-hour break, which I'm sure is good for her. Her sleep seems almost peaceful.

I know no such sleep. When I can finally steal a few hours, heavy brown fire-resistant cotton duck coveralls invade my dreams, dancing around me in a fiery hell that seems only too real. There has to be an end to this order! I begin to wonder if I'll ever be able to hold a pen again in my crippled, spasmed hand.

And then we find out why we're getting special

attention from Little Boss. Big Boss struts in with two slick-looking Chinese men dressed in suits and ties, their hair oiled back from their faces. Ushi is not with them. Hawa is. We've wondered what happened to her. Now we know. She's still "Kitten." She follows behind them in a new outfit, as short and skimpy as before.

The group is near enough that I hear Big Boss trying to explain how difficult it is to work with the material, why it's taking more time than he promised.

"We paid you for a rush order. You charged us. We paid in advance. Now you don't deliver," one man says, gesturing with his arm in disgust.

The other man points to the bolts of material lined against the wall. "All that. Yet to be cut and processed. Why didn't you at least warn us if you couldn't deliver? It's pretty late to be telling us that now."

Big Boss looks stricken as the men move aside for a private conversation. I see him look at Hawa with annoyance. Apparently she was brought along to distract them, and it's obviously not working. I'm sure he wishes he'd brought Ushi instead. She has her ways of making things happen.

I'm watching Hawa, wondering if I can find any compassion or sympathy for her, standing there in her cute little outfit, looking out of place and rather miserable. It's then that I see a miraculous transformation—a performance that would win accolades on any stage or screen. She becomes taller, older. No longer seventeen, but twenty-seven. And imperious. Cold, calculating, and invincible.

She picks up a leg piece from one of the cut piles and walks to the men. "Honorable sirs," she says in a voice strong enough to command the whole factory, "you chose remarkable material. It will protect your workers well, but it is difficult to work with." She holds the piece out in front of her. Pulls on it, demonstrating its firmness. She encourages them to touch it, to test it. "It is difficult to cut. We have had to limit the time of our excellent cutters so they can rest their hands. To rush them would have resulted in second-rate work, and we will not compromise the quality of our product."

Hawa has their attention. They are now holding the leg between them. Pulling on it. Seeing that it is firm. *Impossible to cut!* I want to holler out, but don't. They nod, purse their lips as if in agreement, and return the leg to her—and perhaps for the first time actually look at her. She is quite untouchable. Right now she owns the factory. I look over at Big Boss, who stands there sweating. His hands are hovering, as if he should do something but has no idea what.

"Then, honorable sirs," Hawa goes on, "unfortunately the sewing machines that we had—that have turned out such satisfactory work in the past—were not able to handle the density of this material." Again she holds the leg out in front of them. "Production was slowed until Mr. Lee installed his new, top-of-the-line machines, which now easily accommodate the task." Hawa backs away slightly. Her quick glance at Boss Lee somehow gets him trotting over to join the group.

"Yes, yes," he says as he holds a low bow, which I'm sure he feels shows his great humility. When he bobs up he has that hideous look of controlled geniality on his face. "In one week," he continues, "we will absolutely have this order finished and on its way to you. I apologize deeply for any inconvenience this has caused. I know you will be very pleased with the product we deliver to you." He bows again, deeply.

The two men more or less shrug. What else can they do? Big Boss already has their money, and they need the coveralls. They don't bow back, which I think is not a good sign.

"Perhaps, Mr. Lee, since the honorable sirs now understand the situation, it would be best to get away from the heat of the factory floor." Hawa is still imperious. Still in charge. "I will see that samples of the finished coveralls are brought to the office for them to examine."

"A fine idea," Big Boss says, bowing and bobbing. "Yes, and we can talk further about this at my club. I believe you will find that an enjoyable place to discuss the matter."

The two men are now looking at Hawa, not Big Boss. "Will your charming assistant be joining us?" one of the men asks.

"Oh yes," Big Boss answers quickly.

And I look on in astonishment as Hawa transforms herself again from the haughty, untouchable princess into a cute little kitten.

Twenty-Three

I SEE HER FIRST. "Don't look now, but the dyed-haired shopper friend of Hawa's is lurking around the corner. I'm sure she's spying on us." Mikray and Gulnar walk beside me in the warren of streets across from the factory. We don't change pace, but Mikray leads us in another direction—away from the black café.

"Let's take Quin Fong on a shopping tour. What shall we buy today?" Mikray asks.

Neither Gulnar nor I answer. We came with only one thing on our minds—to get to the café. The little money we have will buy precious time on a computer. Even if we were paid, that's the only thing we would be interested in.

"We could look at food," I say. "I'd consider buying some if I had money."

We pass the video shop and racks of cheap blouses and plastic shoes. We can't even make ourselves stop and pretend to buy.

"Tea would be nice," Gulnar says, and I can almost hear the tears in her voice. Finally, after endless weeks of grueling work with fire-resistant duck, Big Boss has given us time off. Our day will be ruined if we're followed.

"If I remember right, we're near the park. Just a couple

more turns," Mikray says in a loud voice. She pulls at the sleeves of our blouses. Draws us nearer to her. "Don't say anything you don't want her to hear," she whispers. "She's following more closely, more openly. I don't think she knows we've seen her."

We stroll casually as if we're enjoying the sun, which we are. It's a lovely October day.

There are men in the park, clustered around two players who sit on foldout stools, bent over an old wooden game board. An unused board sits on top of a crate under the tree.

"How about a game of *xiangqi*?" Mikray says as she leads us to the tree.

"I don't know how to play," I say.

"I don't either," Gulnar echoes.

"I'll teach you, only it's best we don't move the pieces. Someone may be in the middle of a game, and interfering is a serious offense." We squat around the deserted board, Mikray positioning herself so she's facing the direction we just came from. "Our follower is trying to hide among the women shopping for rice and wilted vegetables, only she's far too pale-purple colored and frilly to blend in." Mikray frowns as her eyes focus back on the board. "You may have a long lesson. Our spy can't seem to decide what rice to buy.

"So, getting back to the game of *xiangqi*, what we want to do here is to get rid of our enemy's general and then the game is over. But, as you can see, the red army is already winning, having captured most of the black army's cannons and chariots and horses. Here we are, lowly black soldiers, and at the moment I don't have a plan for the next move. Do you?" Mikray's lips are drawn tight against her teeth as she says this.

Gulnar and I shake our heads. We all lean over the board.

"Hey, what are you doing? Don't touch that game." The two men who have been watching the players at the other game board hurry toward us.

"We're just looking," Mikray says to them, but we jump to our feet. Mikray shrugs her shoulders, meets them head-on. "We think the one of you with the black pieces is in trouble."

"Yeah? Well, that's none of your business. How about you get out of here? You don't belong in this neighborhood." The men move in closer. "What are you doing here anyway?"

"We work at the factory across the highway, Hubei Work Wear. We're with that one. The one over there buying rice," Mikray calls out in her loudest voice, pointing. "You must know her, right? She's shopping for our lunch."

Everyone looks. For a moment the dyed-haired one stands frozen. Then starts to back away, bumping into the vegetable stands, the bags of rice. She turns away. Gestures to the shop owner, who brings a scoop and starts filling a bag.

The men quiz each other. "I don't know that one. Do

you?" They shrug. Go back to their gaming table. Squat beside it.

If we had a plan, it's now changed. I turn to say something to Mikray—and she's not there. She was right behind Gulnar and me—and now . . .

I grasp Gulnar's hand. "Mikray's gone!" My words come out in a choked whisper. The men don't care, but I'm sure our spy does. "She just disappeared. I don't see her in any of the alleys," I whisper. Our hands are trembling. I don't know what to do. But I know what not to do. *Don't run after her,* I tell myself. *You'll get caught. Mikray is clever enough to get away.*

Our spy is now paying for her purchase. "Let's pretend we're watching the game. The pale-purple one will only see our backs. She might not notice right away that Mikray is missing."

I keep stealing quick glances at the market, glad our spy doesn't blend in. "She's paid. Moving away from the store." When I look again she's at the corner. "She's a pretty bad spy," I say. "She's peeking around a building as if she's somehow hidden from our sight. No. Wait. She's on her way over."

Gulnar and I unclutch our hands, stare blankly at the game.

"Hi, girls," the pale-purple one says, coming up to us. "Having fun on your day off?"

I take a deep breath so I won't pull every dyed strand of hair from her skull and strangle her. I smile sweetly and don't say that standing, hungry, in a baked-clay park with my friend gone, disappeared maybe forever, is not really fun. "Let's move away so we don't disturb the men," I say instead.

"So . . . wasn't there another girl with you before?" she asks. Apparently she's not really interested in whether or not we're having fun.

"You mean Mikray?" I ask, still smiling.

The pale-purple one puts her finger to her lips, chews on her nail as if trying to recall if that might be the name of the missing person. "I guess so," she says. "I'm not really sure of her name."

"Umm," I say, nodding my head a little, very politely.

"Well . . . ah . . . do you know where she went?" The pale-purple one smiles, but she's not as good at it as I am. I think she'd like to strangle me.

"She went off to see if she could find some cheap food. She has a few yuan. We're really hungry." I pause. Her eyes scan the streets and paths leading into the park. I have to keep her here. Give Mikray more time.

"We saw you following us. Thought you might want to join us. Then, when you bought the rice, we hoped you lived near here—and might invite us to lunch. When Mikray comes back, we'll have a little something to offer you in return." I look right at her now. At her empty hands. "But I see you no longer have the rice." I try to look disappointed. "I guess we were wrong, that it wasn't for us."

"Yeah, guess not," she says with a hideous mocking

laugh as she glares at us. Her eyes turn cold and mean. "You can't protect her. We'll find her. You can be sure of that." She jerks her head around. Pulls out her smartphone. Takes a second to check the passageways, then takes off at a run.

Please, Allah, help Mikray escape—find her way across the border so she can be with her family.

The pangs in my heart tell me that whether she escapes or not, I'll never see my friend again.

Twenty-Four

GULNAR AND I stand against the wall where the dyed-haired one—the informer, now so clearly identified—was minutes before. My eyes scan the pathways. To see Mikray will mean she's been caught. To see pale-purple hair will mean our spy abandoned her search for Mikray and decided to return to Ushi with a prize: two other Uyghurs who can be accused of some crime, like trying to steal a game board from Chinese men in the park.

"Roshen?" Gulnar touches my arm.

I look at her. She expects me to make the next move.

And so does Mikray. Her voice—loud and clear—rings in my head. *Wake up, poor Roshen, it is enough to sleep!* she cries out to me. Mikray won't let me forget our poet's call. *Now you have nothing, the only thing to lose is your life.*

They've taken away my freedom, but I will not let them take from me what I hold most dear. My family. My future with Ahmat. The life we've chosen to live together. My hand goes to my necklace, hidden under the soft cotton of my blouse—the blouse I was wearing when he gave me the gift. I desperately want to go back to that day. I close my eyes and try to feel again the awkward touch of his fingers.

Instead, what I feel now is the tremor of Gulnar's hand on my arm, and too quickly I'm forced back to reality. My hand covers hers. "Somehow," I say, "you and I will find the black café. We can't spend the rest of our day cowering in fear. Come," I urge her, "we'll walk in the shadows."

We easily remember how to get to the teahouse. "If we stand at the entrance, maybe we'll have some memory of the direction to the café." We agree we came from the right, only that leaves us with a choice of alleys and one main street we know we didn't use. "We'll try each alley, see where it leads or if anything seems familiar. If not, we'll come back and start over."

Finally we find a square we remember, and again must choose among several alleys. "Are we lost?" Gulnar asks. "The café seemed so close to the teashop when we were with Mikray."

"I hope not," I say. Again we go pathway by pathway, until at last we see the green curtain. A child's toy cart is still parked near the entrance. Next to it is a motorcycle.

With a nod to each other, we part the green curtain and enter. The same man as before stands behind a table cluttered with an old computer and computer parts. For a moment his face freezes.

"Your computer isn't ready yet," he says too loudly. "Come back in two hours." Noises from the back room grow louder and nearer as his hands slice the air, gesturing toward the door.

We turn. Run. Go down the nearest alley. Then into

a small alley leading off from that. Laundry dangles from clotheslines strung over our heads. Bicycles, kids' toys, construction debris litter the path. We stop when we find a large sheet hung out to dry from a second-story window.

"Let's stay here," I say. The sheet offers some protection as we paste our bodies against the wall. Two children, squatting nearby, stop digging in the dirt with sticks and look at us, then go on with their play. "I think we're all right. No one seems to be following us." I look at Gulnar, whose face is ashen white. "What do you think happened back there?" I ask her.

She shakes her head. I don't tell her that I think Mikray and the young man from the factory might be involved in the commotion. I pray that it isn't so. The call made by Quin Fong could have released a network of spies who might know exactly where we are now.

Suddenly I don't even care. I sink to the ground, so tired I can't keep my eyes open. "Check the sun, Gulnar. Let me know when two hours are up. I hope by then I'm brave enough to go back to the café." I hear my own words. I've spoken to her in Mandarin! Tears water my cheeks. They've caged my body. Now my mind, too?

———

Gulnar shakes my arm. When I open my eyes, I know from the length of the shadows that more than two hours has passed. There are more children playing in the street. A few glance over when I start to move.

"It's all right," Gulnar says. "They're our friends. We've been singing songs together, very quietly so we wouldn't wake you. I told them we were resting after a long journey and found it peaceful here in their neighborhood. A couple of their parents came by to check and seemed to judge us harmless. They brought us water." Gulnar unscrews a cap and hands a bottle to me. I gulp it down greedily, not realizing how thirsty I am. The children watch, giggle when I wipe the dribble from my chin.

The children follow us to the end of the short alley. Gulnar's finger goes to her lips to keep them from calling loud goodbyes as we walk away through the maze of alleys that lead to the green curtain.

The motorcycle is no longer beside the toy cart. We stand outside for a moment. Listen. It's quiet. We part the curtain.

The computer man greets us as if he's seeing us for the first time. We give him our few yuan and he leads us through the doors to the back room. I wonder why I trust him. This could be a trap set up by Ushi. There's no escape. No window. No back door.

The sweat that trickles down my body and stains my blouse is from fear as well as the heat of the airless room. Still, I go to the computer and quickly key in the password. If I can just read a few of Ahmat's messages, send him a few of the words that flood my mind before I'm caught.

His messages no longer fill the screen. They're short. Desperate. Attempts to be clever—to disguise our messages in familiar lines from poems, in metaphors of wind and water—are gone. *Wind?* becomes *Are you all right? You must tell me!* He knew the meaning of the fragmented line of poetry I sent him. He knows my despair.

I can't let that be. Has he already gone to the cadre to find out where I am? I've not told him. He must never know. Has he gone to Father? Will they try to come and find me?

I gasp. I need more air to clear my head. I didn't mean to get Father and Ahmat in trouble. If Father complains and tries to bring me home, the cadre will take our land. Or worse. He and Ahmat could disappear as Mikray's father did, and Gulnar's fiancé.

I pull in short, quick breaths. Force my fingers to the keys.

All is well, I write. *Please don't worry. It's nothing but work, work, work. We've been so busy, but what we're doing is very important. We have been making fire-retardant work clothes for men who are in harm's way on their jobs. Most of my time off I must sleep and take care of myself. Today is a full day of rest and I am able to send word. Please let my family know I'm all right.*

My heart still pounds as my shaky hands hover over the keyboard, waiting for me to think up the next lie.

I add a truth. *The girls I am with offer great comfort to me.* Then I quickly search Ahmat's messages again. He says that the crops on the farm are good this summer. I write how wonderful this is and that I can almost taste a delicious fresh carrot from our garden.

Then, because I fear my time is almost up, I write again. *Please don't worry. Please, please don't worry.* Then I add, *I miss everyone, very much. I especially miss you. I wear my reddish-orange blouse today, and remember.*

Truth and falsehood intertwine. I add another. *All is well. I'll send word whenever I can.* And I know it might be impossible to get here again. Hidden cameras. Spies. Too many troubling things are happening. Why did I trust the computer man? He has no reason to be kind to us. Again my breath comes in short, uneven gasps. Air. I need air. I sign off. I must get out of here while I can still move and think about what to do. Gulnar is bent over the keyboard. I tap her shoulder and point to the door.

Gulnar holds up her hand. "Not yet," she whispers. "I need another minute."

She won't leave, but I go. The computer man isn't in his workroom. I peek around the curtain. He's two meters away, talking to someone on a motorcycle. The factory boy, Chen. Was he a false friend to Mikray? A spy for Ushi who helped to get Mikray in trouble so she'd be arrested? Has Mikray already been captured and Chen sent to track us down because we're in this illegal place? Because we're Mikray's friends?

I inch back into the dim light of the computer room and stand against the wall. No one notices. They're alone with their machines. I have time to think, but tight bands around my head make me dizzy. There's no escape. I know that. I can't run as Mikray did. If I could, where would I go? Home?

I grasp my jade necklace. I won't let go of it no matter what they do with me.

It seems forever before the computer man comes into the room and beckons me. He taps Gulnar on the shoulder. We follow him out of the room.

"Thank you for coming," he says in a calm, pleasant voice. He parts the curtain for us. There is no motorcycle, no factory boy outside.

Something is being put into my hand. I clasp my fingers around it.

I can't keep from looking at the man who gave me the paper.

He gives a tiny nod. Shoos us away.

I grab Gulnar's arm and lead her around a corner to a narrow alley. I open my palm. A tiny piece of paper is wrapped inside a yuan note. I open the paper.

Remember this before you swallow it. Hotan dates and nuts. Local bus #56 north down the main road to Taikang Lu, walk 2 blocks west past Hankou Clothing, then . . .

Mikray has told us how to reach the Uyghur man who can help if we need to escape.

Twenty-Five

Y OU LEFT HERE with Mikray. Where is she now?" Ushi grabs Gulnar and me the minute we walk through the door and marches us up the stairs to her office, shouting loud enough for everyone in the factory to hear. "Did she run off?"

I tell myself to be calm. Mikray would be proud if I stay composed and *sweet*. I must remember my secret weapon.

I bow my head slightly so I don't have to look directly at her. "We were hoping you might know." I pause.

Ushi tightens her grip on my arm.

"You see . . . a girl from the factory . . . the one with the purple hair . . . she was at the same park where we were. She was buying rice and we thought, I guess we really hoped, that she lived in the neighborhood and might invite us to lunch. She'd been so good to Hawa and her friends, we thought maybe she'd do something nice for us." I'm talking faster and faster as Ushi's face gets red and seems about to burst.

"Mikray had a few yuan. She went off to see if she could find something to offer in return . . . in case we were asked. Then the girl followed Mikray. We thought she was going after her." I shake my head slowly. "We waited and waited, but neither of them came back. We hoped they might be here at the factory." I lift my head now to look into Ushi's eyes. I try to have a tear roll down my face, but I can't make it happen. "Has the Chinese girl returned? Or are they both lost?" I furrow my brow in an effort to match my pathetic voice.

"You're useless," Ushi says, dropping my arm, pushing me away. "Sit. Until you remember where she's gone."

She turns to Gulnar. Drags her under the light. "How about you? What did you do all day?"

Gulnar, who spends countless hours with no expression on her face as she embroiders her endless tapestry, leaves her face blank. "I do not speak good Mandarin," she replies, her voice as emotionless as her face. She has answered in perfect Mandarin, far superior to Ushi's.

Ushi raises her hand above her head and slaps Gulnar across the face, almost knocking her off her feet.

I rush to her.

"Leave her alone," Ushi orders.

I fall back. Muscles taut. Eyes flaring before I remember to *be sweet*. "Please," I plead, "let me interpret for her. I'm certain she'll tell you all she knows."

"Aaaah," Ushi snarls. "You're both useless." She stomps to an inside door. Opens it. "Come on in," she says.

Quin Fong and Chen walk into the room.

I clutch the back of the chair. I was certain it was Chen who brought Mikray's note to me at the café. Gave it to the computer man to pass on—but he really *is* Ushi's spy!

You trusted him, Mikray. So I did too! The words seethe in my brain as I look at the traitor. He must know exactly where Mikray is. Ushi must know. And they've trapped us. They'll make me tell what was in the note. Maybe they already know and think we're trying to escape. Now three Uyghur girls will be sent for reeducation or to jail or wherever they send you so you're never heard from again.

"We'll just stand here until one of you comes up with a good idea of where she's hiding," Ushi announces.

I draw in a quick breath. Ushi turns toward me, but by then my mouth is closed. I try to absorb this new information without looking too confused. I can't keep myself from stealing a glance at the motorcycle boy. He slouches, arms folded across his chest. Looks bored.

"We know she didn't leave town." Ushi spits out the words as if the very thought of Mikray disgusts her. "Every policeman around here is looking for her. Her brother and mother are missing. The authorities are not going to let her get away."

"If the police haven't found her yet, how were we supposed to?" motorcycle boy asks.

"It was up to you to trail her," the pale-purple-haired one says. "I called you the minute she disappeared."

She's lying. She walked into the park to talk to Gulnar and me before she made a phone call. She's a bad spy and is blaming Chen.

I watch him shift from one foot to the other as Ushi

quizzes him. "It's a poor neighborhood," he says. "Lots of places to hide. I can keep looking if you want me to, but the police will do a better job. They can go into houses and search."

Ushi goes to the desk. Sits. Cradles her head. Rubs her forehead. Her eyes are slits of hatred when she looks up. "The authorities gave us the job of keeping track of her. You're both paid good money to do just that. Maybe it's time to find someone else. Get out of my sight," she says, flipping her hand at them. "You're useless."

I step beside Gulnar. We back toward the door.

"Oh no. Not you two. I'm not done with you yet." Ushi sits back in her chair. She doesn't say anything, just sits there.

I put on a neutral expression and examine the room. It's a barren place. A couple of file cabinets, a wastebasket. The window is open, letting in fresh air that's far superior to what we breathe on the factory floor. Ushi still stares. I'm not certain what she's waiting for us to do.

I look around again. Concrete walls, concrete floors, three doors—one leading to the stairway and the factory, one that Ushi's spies just used, and another that must lead to Big Boss's office. I wonder where Hawa is. Where she is working.

"Are you ready to tell me where your friend went?" Ushi is alert again, sitting straight up in her chair, her words snappish, hard.

I shrug. "She didn't return. We didn't dare to go looking for her. I think she might have lost her way." I stop talking. There's another long silence.

"Tell me about your friend Mikray. Why did she come here?"

"As I remember from when we first came, she said she was on the local cadre's list and had no choice. It was the same with me," I say. "The cadre told my father I was selected and that I had to come."

"Did she have friends around here?"

"This is the second time we've been away from the factory since we've been here. We're not allowed to have phones. How could any of us make friends?" My voice rises as the words tumble out. I'm tired and hungry.

"You're angry, I see," Ushi says. She puts her elbows on the table. Leans toward me. "Now maybe we're getting somewhere. So, what did you do after your friend left? I hear you didn't stay in the park."

My mind freezes. I'm too tired to be clever and I don't know how Mikray's note got to me, only that it was her handwriting and only she could know about the swallowing. I don't know if the motorcycle boy is a spy or if he really is Mikray's friend. And I don't know if Gulnar and I were followed by someone who told Ushi exactly what we did all day—that we went to an illegal café. Does she know all this, and is she trying to trick us into some confession?

We are more innocent than she can imagine.

"There is no shade in the park," I find myself saying. "We waited there for a long time, then sought refuge in a nearby alley, sitting under a canopy of drying laundry. I fell asleep."

"It was a quiet place, children playing in the street." Gulnar takes over my narrative. "Roshen slept, I played and sang with children. It reminds me of home. A good way to spend a day off. People were kind. They bring water. It was refuge all day." She stops. Wipes pretend sweat from her brow, or maybe it's real. It's probably hard for her to speak flawed Mandarin.

"Please, may we go to room. We're hungry. We don't want to miss supper. We need good night's sleep to be ready for work tomorrow." Gulnar's voice is soft, soothing. It should charm the meanest old ox. But not Ushi.

"Good try," Ushi says. "However, I'm hungry too." She looks at her watch. "Just get the hell out of here. I've got bigger worries than you right now."

Our arms go around each other as we slowly turn and exit, using all the restraint we can find not to flee up the stairs.

There is no line outside the kitchen when we get to our floor.

"Grab a bowl," I say to Gulnar. Hunger has quickly overridden my fear.

Cook is still standing behind her pot. "Not many are

eating tonight," she says, dipping a ladle into whatever concoction of cheap food she's prepared. "I'll give you extra." And she does. My bowl overflows with potatoes, onions. . . . The smell of pork hits my nostrils.

"No," I cry. "No. Not tonight." Tears blind my eyes as I drag my body down the hallway, Gulnar at my side. We push through the toilet-room door and dump the food down the hole in the nearest stall.

There's barely a glance in our direction as we go into our room. It's quiet except for Zuwida's cough, which has come back. She's getting thinner, and I'm sure she went without supper. How I wish I had sweet dates and nuts in my pocket to give her.

I climb to my top bunk. When I look out, I see a room full of eyes staring at me—at me, at the lower bunk, and then back at me.

I bow my head. Shake it.

Twenty-Six

I INCH OVER to the edge of my bunk and stare at empty space. Three weeks have passed since Mikray vanished into a warren of streets. Her sheet, notebook, pencil—all her belongings—are gone. But no one can erase Mikray. She's in my heart, my mind, my being, and always will be.

Would she and I have been friends if we had met in Hotan—Mikray a woman working in a man's world, me a teacher? The answer is probably not, even if our paths had crossed in some inexplicable way. I'd be busy trying to preserve our literary heritage; she'd be busy helping run the family trade, assuming her father had not "disappeared."

Does Chen know what happened to Mikray? If he does, he's not telling. He turns away when I look at him, maybe afraid of getting caught by Ushi in his own double role. I try not to think the worst. I pray she has escaped across the border or is at least hiding until she can.

I stare at her empty bed. Curious that no one has claimed it. Was the life force of Mikray so strong that a secret *keep off* signal radiates from the plywood? Or—I pause a moment, let my mind wrap around my next thought—am *I* that powerful? Is there something about me that keeps them from taking it? Maybe I am, because no one else will sleep in Mikray's bed while I'm here. I wouldn't let them. Its emptiness is my "wake up" call.

Our lunch break is over and everyone heads for the stairs. We're fewer than before. It wasn't only Mikray who didn't return. Twelve Chinese girls fled, hoping to find a job at an industrial park in some city where there's a chance for decent wages and hours — or to return to their homes. That leaves forty-six of us to do the work of sixty. New girls begin to trickle in, mostly from the nearby countryside, where they are used to hard work on a family rice paddy or peanut farm. Which is good, because we're working sixteen, sometimes eighteen hours a day making cheap uniforms for nurses — short sleeves, three pockets, eight buttonholes. Lightweight polyester and cotton material. We no longer have to work in shifts. We're back to our old schedule.

I'm tired of the color peach. There aren't many bolts of that left stacked against the wall. Only piles of blue and green. I wonder which nurse is better, a peach one or a blue one. I have yet to decide when a subliminal buzz goes around the cutting tables telling me it's energy-tea time. The Chinese girls think the boy who wheels the cart is cute. When Little Boss isn't looking, he stops and flirts with them, fondles their hands when he gives them their little paper cups of tea. He's learned not to touch Jemile, but I think he wants to. I've watched him studying her face, liking what he sees. Does he sense the pure innocence of her being? Or does he just like her looks, different from what he's used to? He pays no attention to me. I long ago sent out a *do not touch* signal, and it seems to have worked.

The buzz stops. I look up and know why. The cart is not wheeled by the boy this afternoon. Chen is pushing it, and he's not stroking the Chinese girls' hands. He barely gives them time to take the cup, drink, and return it.

He stops in front of me. When I reach for the cup, I look right at him. Try to make him look at me. I want to scream, *Give me some sign! Did Mikray escape? Is she in prison? What happened?* He tries too hard not to look at me. I don't know if that's good or bad.

I see his body tense when I pour the tea down the table leg and make a tiny puddle on the floor. He missed the part where I pretend-drank with my other hand. He's already pushing the cart away when I reach out to return the cup. He grabs it. Keeps moving.

For a moment my hand is too shaky to hold the scissors. Is it better that I still don't know anything? Was he really Mikray's friend? Will he help me if I need him?

Why is he still here?

Slowly I let the crunch of scissors, the loud drone of the sewing machines pervade my mind.

Place the pattern. *Crrrunch,* release, *crrrunch,* release, *crrrunch,* release. Turn scissors. *Crrrunch,* release, *crrrunch,* release, *crrrunch,* release. Soon I'm beating the rhythm with my toes to remind them they're part of my body. The part that went numb a few hours ago.

It's eight o'clock. Time for our newly initiated supper break. They finally noticed that dinner is of little interest to us at ten or midnight when we can't stay awake. Cutters go first, maybe because we're nearest the door. We get fifteen minutes to eat, then back to work, and sewers go up for their fifteen minutes; then finishers get their turn.

I pee, get my bowl, and stand in line. We haven't been served pork again since returning from our day off. Maybe Ushi told Cook not to, that she needs the Uyghur girls to eat and keep healthy until they hire more workers. If it is a kind gesture from Ushi—to keep her indentured Uyghur girls from starving to death, now she needs us so badly —it's welcomed. It finally makes sense to me why Big Boss and Ushi went to the trouble of getting us here. Not so much fulfilling a duty to the government as assuring themselves a steady work force. We're the only ones who don't have the privilege of leaving when they unlock the doors. No, that isn't entirely true. We can escape and hide somewhere for the rest of our lives if we choose to.

The least they can do is give us food we can eat. I remind myself that we pay for it. That these pitiful meals are being deducted from the salaries we have yet to receive.

I scoop food into my mouth as I go down the hallway. Manners, politeness seem unimportant when you're hungry. The chicken is half chewed when I go through the door to our room and see Zuwida on her bunk. She shouldn't be here. Finishing girls are the last to eat—and she's alone. If she'd stayed here after lunch, they would have come and dragged her back to work. Being sick and weak is not an excuse for not working.

I put my bowl on Mikray's bunk and go to her as quietly as I can. If she's sleeping and somehow got away with it, I don't want to disturb her. She's curled up, facing the wall. I touch her arm and know right away that she has a fever.

"Zuwida," I call to her as softly as I can. "Please talk to me. Tell me what's happening." I'm leaning over her now. Her eyes flutter.

Then I see it. Blood has drained from her mouth onto her bed.

Jemile is beside me now. "Get a cold cloth for her head. Quick. She's burning up."

Zuwida tries to raise her head. "I . . . I need . . ." Her words turn into a fit of coughing. She sinks to the bed again, her body twisted in pain.

"Hold the cloth to her head. Try to calm her. I'm going to get Ushi. Someone who can help. She should be in the hospital."

I run to the forbidden zone, to Ushi's office, and I pound on the door. Pound and pound. There's no answer. I pound on Big Boss's door. Still no answer. I don't know where else to look. I run into the factory, past cutting and the sewing machines. Zuwida's little boss is sitting at her desk. "You have to do something," I say. "Zuwida is very ill with fever and cough. She should be in a hospital."

I'm met with annoyance. Little Boss's hands wave in the air as she tries to calm me. "I know. I know," she says. "She fainted. I had her taken to her bed."

"She needs a doctor!" I'm shouting at her.

She looks at me and smiles. "I'll take care of it," she says in a mocking voice.

"Please. Oh please do," I say in my sweetest, nicest voice, reminding myself that more is accomplished that way.

I rush back upstairs. Jemile and I stay with Zuwida, taking turns bringing more cold cloths to lay on her body. Our fifteen minutes are up, but we do not leave until Adile is there to stay with Zuwida. "I have asked her little boss to call a doctor," I say. "She must have help. I've left the broth from my supper. Please give it to her."

Adile closes her eyes for a moment as she brushes her fingers through Zuwida's hair. "We must pray for her," she says, bowing her head.

Jemile and I return to the factory. When the sewing girls appear, Adile is not with them. I don't know what that means. Fifteen minutes after that the finishing girls return. This time Adile is with them, walking beside her little boss, her jaw clenched so tight I think she might break her teeth.

It is Gulnar who makes eye contact. *No doctor. Not yet,* she mouths in Uyghur. Then she folds her hands, lays them on her cheek, and tilts her head. Zuwida is sleeping. I try to think this is a good sign.

It is midnight before the machines are shut down. I pry my hand open enough to drop the scissors and dash for the stairs, along with nine other Uyghur girls.

Zuwida is not there. Her bunk is empty. All that is left is the bloodstain.

Twenty-Seven

THERE IS SOME kind of package on my bunk when I crawl into bed. The light in the room is off, but enough light filters in from the hallway for me to see an envelope on top of the package. I don't like it. Someone could be tricking me—leaving something that's been stolen on my bed. The dyed-haired spy. I made her look stupid.

There is no way I can sleep without opening the mysterious package and reading the note. If my eyes were half-closed for the last few hours of work, they're wide-open now.

When it is completely quiet in the hallway, I hide the letter under my nightclothes and sneak to the stairway that leads to the factory floor, where there is no monitor to watch me open the unsealed envelope. The message inside is written in perfect Mandarin.

Zuwida died. Her body is being prepared for burial tomorrow. You are her family. No one else can be there with her. Bus fare is enclosed for all nine of you. Directions are attached. Put on your work smocks, eat breakfast, go to the factory floor just before seven. Go down the stairs to

the first floor, to the sign-out desk. No one will be there.
The door to the outside will be unlocked. A person will be
waiting for you at the last bus stop.

The factory cannot make its delivery date without your
help. You will be let back in.

May Allah be with you and our beautiful sister.

I lean hard against the wall. It holds me up but does not share its strength with me. It has to be Hawa who sent the note, but why to me and not to her devoted sycophants? And why in Mandarin? "Please, Allah," I whisper, "bring to my being the courage I need to do this, for I do not recognize the strength others see in me."

I must wake everyone and tell them. I go to Adile first. Shake her shoulders until she finally rouses. "What?" she cries out. I clasp my hand over her mouth and wait for silence to settle again. "It's Zuwida," I whisper. "She died, Adile." I grasp her hands. Hold them tightly in mine. "Hawa sent word and money so we can all go to prepare her for burial. Only," I add, "I'm not certain it was Hawa— the note is not signed. It's best we don't mention her name." I tell Adile the details. "Please help me let everyone know. It must be secret among us, and we all must go."

"Tomorrow morning we'll tell them, Roshen. They're too deep in sleep now."

We sit side by side for a while before I climb back to my bunk.

I open the package and find nine white scarves and a

white shrouding cloth. The package is much too big to sneak out. Each of us must hide a scarf. The only way I can think of to carry the shrouding cloth is to wrap it around my body and put my work smock over it. Can I do that? Will the sacredness of the *kafan* be lost if it touches my body?

My mother could answer my questions. She leaves us from time to time to go to the home of a relative who has died. It is women who wash and shroud the bodies of other women in preparation for burial. Mother knows the ritual. She knows prayers. I've caught her praying, her lips moving, no sound coming out, standing barefoot or kneeling on a cloth, facing Mecca. She is afraid my sister or I might display some knowledge of religion and attract the unwanted attention of the authorities if we see her, so she worships secretly. No religion is to be taught in the home, only in mosques, where women aren't allowed to go.

Oh, Mother, why didn't you trust me with our prayers? I need prayers now to comfort me. To send Zuwida on to the life of happiness she deserves. *Aren't our prayers a part of who I am, of who you want me to be?* My question hangs silently and angrily in the air. Anger at myself, at Mother, for letting such awful people rule our lives.

Father trusted me with the words of our poets. Why didn't Mother trust me with our prayers?

I find no comfort in sleep because no sleep comes for a long time. Exhaustion must have overtaken me, and I wake only when Adile touches my arm. The sun has risen, and I see she has already told many of the girls. They watch as I blink my eyes open to the reality of the day.

The overwhelming thought that it's a trick, that some traitor wishes us all to disappear, floods my mind, but that's not useful thinking. I nod reassuringly. Climb down from my bunk. Check to see that the hallway outside our door is clear and reach for the white scarves that have been left for us. *There is one for each of us,* I mouth in Uyghur. *Hide it until we are with Zuwida.*

I let Adile wake the rest of the girls while I put on my smock and go to the toilet. I splash water on my face and don't mind that it trickles down my arms, my body. It will dry while I stand in line for breakfast.

We seldom talk in the morning. Today we try hard not to say anything to one another, and that is a very different thing. The Chinese girls ignore us as always, so they don't notice, not even the pale-purple-haired one. She's giggling over a photo with a friend.

I eat my watery porridge. Wash my bowl. Climb back onto my bunk and unwrap the shrouding cloth. If I sit against the wall and lift my smock, I may be able to wind it around my body so no one will notice. It's a very long piece of material. I stretch it out, find the middle, and place it against my back. Bringing the two ends forward, I cross the material under my breasts, around again to the back, then front, then back, until I am bound all the way down to my hips. I have no way to fasten the ends, so I tie them in a strong knot. I've wound myself so tightly I can hardly breathe. I don't know if it's from lack of air or because I feel like a half-dead mummy. Maybe it's God's punishment for my sacrilege.

And how will I carry the money? The directions? What if the door is locked and Ushi catches us?

I look at the clock. It's time to go. The voice in my head is loud and clear. *You will tie the money and directions in your scarf. You'll hide it in your clothing. Remember how you and Mikray hid the naan when you snuck back into the hotel?* The thought of Mikray fills me with courage. She would be proud of us now. Of me.

The clock is ticking down as I climb from my bunk. "Let's split into groups of three," I say. "Come last, Adile," I whisper to her as I pass. "Make sure everyone comes." I take Jemile and Nurbiya by their arms and pull them with me. Their fear is palpable. I wonder if they'll make it down the stairs. We fall in step with the Chinese girls—everyone rushing now to be checked in to work on time.

Little bosses stand at the door with their pads and pencils. They're half asleep. Jemile, Nurbiya, and I pass behind them unnoticed and head for the next flight of stairs. A few seconds later Gulnar, Rayida, and Nadia join us. When we're halfway down the stairs to the bottom floor, we halt —our eyes glued to the top of the stairs. It's grown too quiet. Then I see Adile, Patime, and Letipe creeping along the wall in the shadow. "Let's go. Keep against the wall. Move quickly," I say in more of a hiss than a whisper.

When I reach the bottom of the steps, I start running and hope everyone follows. The door's in sight. No one is at the desk. I try the handle. It works, and I open the door just enough to squeeze through. "Go across the highway. Hide. We'll regroup there," I whisper as each one passes. Adile is the last to come.

The traffic on the street is heavy, but we all cross safely and huddle together on the other side, shielded from view of the factory by a street merchant's wares.

"There's a bus in fifteen minutes, four long blocks away. We're too exposed if we walk along the highway. We have to find a parallel street," I say, moving away, knowing how easy it is to get lost. Ushi may already have Quin Fong trying to follow us. Or Chen—I still have no idea whose side he's on.

The townspeople stare at us, curiosities for sure—nine Uyghur girls rushing down the street. It's lucky we have sweaters that we brought from home. We wear them in the factory against the November chill that settles into the building overnight. Now they partly conceal the blueness of our uniforms.

I don't feel the chill in the air. The shroud that's wrapped around my body makes me sweat. I wonder again if there will be any sacredness left in it at all.

We find the bus stop. I give each girl a yuan note for bus fare. We try to be inconspicuous. There are few shadowy places to hide.

The bus comes. It's crowded to bursting, but I'm glad to

be riding away from the factory, even for our sad mission. It seems forever before we get to the gate where we are to transfer to another bus, one that takes us into the countryside. I wasn't told what time that bus would arrive, only that it will.

It does. We pay our fare. We each have a seat. Soon we leave big highways for narrow paved roads. Small towns, sometimes just a cluster of a few houses, line our way. I see few cars and trucks. Traffic is most often a bicycle, a motorcycle, or a person walking. It could almost be like home, except there's too much water here—ponds and lakes, endless green fields. And too many thick poles holding up overhead wires.

According to the note in the package, the name of the town we're going to will be on a white vertical sign attached to one of these poles. It will be at a crossroads where there is only one house. Someone will meet us there, and we'll walk to the small town where Zuwida has been taken. I have shared the name with the driver, who assures me he knows where we're going.

We're growing restless. The villages are farther and farther apart, and it feels as though we will never reach our destination.

We're the only passengers on the bus now.

"Roshen." Adile slides into the seat beside me. "It seems too far." She whispers in Uyghur, but everyone hears. They wait for my answer.

"It's okay, I'm sure," I say, even though I'm not certain it is. "Someone at the factory has respect for the dead and made it possible for us to come. We must believe that." I say these words to reassure myself, for it has crossed my mind that the driver might have been told to dump us at the crossroads and no one will be waiting there. "We have return bus fare," I add. "We're expected to come back."

"Hey, you girls speak a funny language." Our Chinese driver turns his head to take a quick look at us, smiles, chuckles. "Why are all of you pretty girls coming out here to the middle of nowhere anyway?" He keeps talking, even though his eyes are back on the road. "I have a lot of friends who would like to meet you if you're going to be staying a while," he says. "I live not too far away."

He seems innocent, flirting with us, not like someone Ushi has paid to deliver us to a detention center—a possibility that has been more and more on my mind. We've been a disappointment to Ushi by running away, by dying . . . by being a favorite of Big Boss.

The driver turns toward us again. Leers.

"We, ah, we're only here for the day. Thank you," I stammer. He shrugs. Keeps driving. I won't ask him how much farther we have to go or if he really knows the road we want. And we can't be sure the place we're going to is safe.

With hand signals and whispers the driver can't possibly hear, we divide into two groups. We no longer look at the countryside. Five of us scan the electric and phone line poles on the right-hand side of the road, and four look for a sign of any kind on the left-hand side.

Even before we see the road sign, the driver is screeching his brakes to a stop. "This is it," he says. He opens the door and we pile out.

The cook who was fired for helping Zuwida is standing by the roadway. She is wearing a white headscarf. There is a soft sadness in her eyes as her arms open to welcome us.

I go to her. I find no words; my throat is choked. My hands cross my heart and I bow my head. I want her to take me in her arms, as she must have taken Zuwida, and tell me that everything will be all right.

One by one the girls follow my gesture, and we all stand before her with tears streaming down our faces.

"Come," she says in Mandarin. "We have much to do."

Twenty-Eight

WALKING DOWN THE mud-puddled road through the harvested fields, I almost feel at home. The sounds, the rhythms of life here are familiar. I hear the hum of insects, not the noisy drone of sewing machines or the roar of traffic. I hear birdcalls, not earsplitting horns.

The dirt road becomes a narrow path. A farmer bends over a small vegetable garden, picking what is ready for today's use, taking it to his handcart at the side of the path. A woman in a distant plot tills the earth with her hoe, preparing the ground for winter planting.

We come to a small cluster of houses. The cook leads us to the back of one. It's a stone house with a slanted, tiled roof. Much of the white plaster that once covered the house has washed away, leaving earth-colored stones exposed. With thick walls, it's a sturdy house that blends in an ageless way into the landscape.

"Please come inside. We will have tea and then I will tell you of the journey Zuwida made."

It is dark inside. The stone walls block out the sunlight, but a small fire burns in the hearth, bringing comforting warmth to the room and to the tiled floor, which we now walk upon in bare feet since we have left our shoes at the door. The room is sparsely furnished, and we're invited to sit on pillows. While the cook prepares tea, we take out the white scarves we've been hiding and tie them around our heads. It is safe now to mourn our friend openly. The paper and the precious yuan I carried hidden go into my pocket.

The cook appears in the doorway with tea and rice cakes and smiles at the sight of us in our scarves. She sits on the floor and ceremoniously offers tea. She fills a bowl, offers it to Adile, looks at her in a way no one has since we arrived at the factory, and bows her head. She does this for each of us. Then she pours her own tea, and we drink together. Rice cakes are passed, and we try to take them without too much greediness.

"Zuwida was finally taken to the hospital on the back of a motorcycle," the cook tells us. "She died two days later. Hawa was able to get in touch with her relatives, but they could do nothing. They are too poor. Perhaps not caring." She stops. Brushes tears away with her fingers. "We are fortunate that Chen has a loving heart. He let Hawa know Zuwida was ill, and he rescued Zuwida's body. She was brought here late last evening. This time she was tied to the back of the motorcycle in an old rice sack."

The binding cloth seems to tighten around me. I gulp air. Swallow. I try to purge the awful image that flashes through my head with thoughts of Chen's kindness.

"Her body is here in your home?" I ask, my voice making unnatural, squeaky sounds. "She is finally at rest?"

"Zuwida is here. Her journey was not pleasant, but she was kept from a far worse fate."

For a moment our host closes her eyes. Her lips move as if in prayer. "My name is Yan Zhi. I am Hui Muslim. I am Chinese, but we are all one under the commands of Allah. I will help you in the bathing and shrouding of the body. The *nu ahong* who lives in a neighboring village has agreed to come to lead us in the prayers for the dead. We are fortunate to have a female imam nearby."

My hands go to my heart and I bow my head, over-whelmed by the kindness, the gentleness of this woman who seems not to notice or care that we are Uyghur.

My hands still touch my heart as I lift my head. "Thank you," I say, and I hear these words echoed by those around me. Yan Zhi's hands go to her heart as she nods in acknowledgment.

"Let's begin," she says.

"I carry the shroud that was given to us on my body. I—I had to," I stammer. "There was no other way to hide it. Will it be all right to use?"

"I believe it will be all the more sacred because it has had your protection. Come, my daughters," Yan Zhi says, rising from the floor. "We will perform our ablutions in the room where I have laid Zuwida's body."

We walk through a door into a dimly lit room. Zuwida's body is on a table. She still wears a hospital gown. Ushi called her Mouse, and she does look tiny lying there, pale, emaciated. There seems so little left of her.

Yan Zhi takes my arm and leads me to a dark corner. Together we unwind the long length of cotton. Yan Zhi folds it into five equal pieces, each long enough to cover Zuwida's body, and cuts the pieces apart. She sprinkles a few drops of flower-scented perfume on the prepared *kafan* and lays it aside.

"Roshen," she says, "will you be first to perform the ritual? The water in the sink is pure. It comes from a deep well."

I'm surprised she knows my name. It pleases me. I go to the sink.

"Wash your hands three times," Yan Zhi says.

I turn the handle on the faucet, and the coolest, most delicious-smelling water flows over my hands. I rub my palms, entwine my fingers. I would gladly wash my hands five times. More. But Yan Zhi is counting. "Now cup your hands. Fill them with water and wash your face, again three times."

The cool water on my face restores my whole body. It is better than a full night's sleep.

"Now take the basin that's on the shelf beside you and fill it with water. Wash your arms up to the elbows, three times, beginning with your right hand. Your feet will be next. Place the basin on the floor and wash each foot up to the ankle, three times."

The joy of cleansing my body with pure water is joined by another awareness: a peacefulness I have not felt in so long. I have finished my ablutions, and Yan Zhi now recites a prayer in Arabic. Somehow I understand the words: "I bear witness that there is no god but Allah alone, without any partner, and I bear witness that Muhammad (peace be upon him) is his servant and messenger." These words bring peace. Perhaps I was taught the prayer when I was a young child.

I squat on the floor and rest as Yan Zhi leads the others, one by one, through their ablutions.

All of us prepare Zuwida's body for burial. Gulnar helps Yan Zhi remove Zuwida's clothes, carefully covering her private parts with small cloths to preserve her modesty. She is turned onto her left side so that the right side of her body can be washed. Three girls help, using soft cloths with soap and water for the first two washes and pure water with scent for the third wash.

Zuwida is turned onto her right side, and three other girls perform the ritual washes. Adile is chosen to wash and braid Zuwida's hair, something she has done for her friend many times before. She also takes a cloth and dries her body.

It is Yan Zhi and I who place the shroud. Five times we cover Zuwida with the pieces of white cotton. Yan Zhi cuts strips of cloth from the top and bottom of the material, and we use them to bind the *kafan* at Zuwida's head and at her feet, careful to tie it in such a way that her head and feet are clearly differentiated. It is important that she is laid in the earth with her face turned right toward the Ka'ba, the House of God at Mecca.

"The nu ahong will be here shortly to lead us in prayer. Let's leave for a moment and refresh ourselves with tea." We sit silently. Drink our tea and eat more rice cakes.

A middle-aged woman arrives with three younger women. They are attired in dark dresses. Large white headscarves cover their hair and their necks. They greet us in the traditional Arabic way.

"At peace?"

"At peace!" we answer. "And you?"

"At peace," they say, finishing the greeting.

"Let us begin our prayers for the deceased," the nu ahong says. "It is important that her body be laid to rest this day before sunset."

The nu ahong stands close to Zuwida's body. Yan Zhi arranges us behind her.

"I am offering prayers for this dead body in compliance with the commands of Allah," the nu ahong says. "Please join me in reciting the supplications."

She recites her prayers in a loud voice. Yan Zhi and the nu ahong's followers join her in softer, lower voices. Five times the prayers are stopped and they say the *takbir*. I know these words. *"Allahu akbar,"* I say with them. "God is most great."

And then it is over. Yan Zhi brings a wide board into the room. The nu ahong and her companions transfer Zuwida's body from the table to the board and cover it with a white sheet.

"The nu ahong has arranged for the burial. Zuwida will be carried to the road, where a car awaits," Yan Zhi says. "She will be taken to their village. The imam there will say the prayers and see that she is properly laid to rest." Yan Zhi turns her eyes away from us. "It is best that your presence in the area is not known."

We stand solemnly by the door as Zuwida's body is carried away. *"Shie-shie,"* we say over and over again to the women. "Thank you."

"Hosh," we whisper in Uyghur to Zuwida. "Goodbye."

We step outside to watch the slow procession. We watch long after they have disappeared from our sight.

My mind fills with questions. Will the authorities allow a Uyghur person to be buried in a Hui burial ground? Won't they have to fill out papers saying who she is? I know I can't ask these questions, that I must not doubt the goodwill and courage of Yan Zhi. And I don't really want to know the answers. I want to think only of Zuwida's peaceful transition into the afterlife.

When we go back inside, Yan Zhi invites us into her kitchen. "You must have at least one good meal while you are away from your homes," she says. And she puts us to work washing and scraping vegetables, cutting fruit. We gladly obey. Soon we're sitting on pillows, eating from her bowls. We do not have to sniff for traces of pork or pick out rotten potatoes.

———

Toward the end of the meal, Yan Zhi goes to her kitchen ledge. She comes back with a platter full of large red dates and then returns to the ledge for a bowl of walnuts. "These gifts," she says, "were brought to me by the same young man who brought Zuwida to me. They are from a friend, he said."

Gulnar and I exchange glances. We know where they are from. We may never know who sent them. But as I fill my mouth with the luscious sweet taste of the date, Mikray is with us. Hawa is too. We are all together once again as we mourn our dear sister.

Twenty-Nine

IT IS LATE AFTERNOON by the time we follow Yan Zhi down the path to the road, where we catch the last bus of the day that will take us to the city gates. I'm not pleased to see the same driver. But his interest in us has passed, and he's annoyed at the time it takes to collect nine fares. He speeds off before we find seats, sending us lurching down the aisle, rudely jarring us into the reality of our return.

I was the last to get on the bus. The others have paired off, leaving me to sit by myself. I study the landscape, the many lakes and streams we drive by. I think of the abundance of water that for weeks saturated the ground. So different from home, where every precious drop of water seems a miracle.

It's not good to think of soil and water. This is the earth in which Zuwida's body has been buried. By now her grave has been dug, her body laid in the ground. However kindly it has been done, her body will be devoured by this earth when it should be preserved by the hot, dry sand of our homeland.

For a moment I feel her shroud tighten around my body. I know it's not there. I know it's been unwound, cut to the right size, rituals carried out as they should be. Yet it became part of my body, and I pray now that this same cloth will somehow protect Zuwida, help to nourish her lingering spirit as she lies in this distant grave.

Please, God, I say in my mind, *look upon the tiny, frail shell of Zuwida's body with mercy. Take her to the next realm with no more suffering.* I wish I knew the prayers that could help her now.

A memory overwhelms me. We were on our journey south, trapped in the van with Ushi. We saw mountains up ahead, our precious Kunlun, and somehow knew that when we passed over them, our lives would forever change. *I am far from my homeland,* I said.

A small voice joined me. *I am a wanderer, the prince of wanderers. I cannot bear this wandering, my face is sallow,* we finished together. It was Zuwida who knew the poetry of our people, and we have left her—this child of our Uyghur land—in a foreign grave.

I don't have prayers. I must leave her body to the will of God, but I can tell her story. If I don't, it will be as if she didn't exist at all.

More and more people get on the bus. They look at me and choose another seat. My Uyghurness and my blue uniform are not inviting. I hope some woman will be bold enough to sit here. I don't want to sit next to a man. Han men seem to like our looks and think it's all right to touch.

If I don't look at them, they won't see me, I tell myself.

I stare out the window and think of weather. The

monsoon rains finally stopped. Now the cold is a worry. We're lucky that today is mild; our sweaters have kept us warm enough.

Someone sits next to me. I don't know if it's a man or woman, and I will not look. My eyes are glued to the passing fields; I think only of Zuwida. Slowly, words come to me. I fit those I need into verse.

> Her body in a cold, wet grave
> Elfin small with big black eyes
> Made a slave for the cause of China.
> Was she fourteen years of age?

The more I see outside the window, the more easily the right words come.

> Lie quiet now in this faraway land
> But sing your desert song, Zuwida,
> Daughter of the Taklamakan.

I say my poem over and over to myself until I feel a hand creep up my leg, above my knee. I turn and swat with all my might. I leap over his legs to the aisle and slide onto the laps of Patime and Letipe. Only then do I look to see a young kid, snickering, laughing at his exploit. Those around him, the grownups, pat him on the back. They think it's funny too.

If I'd had a knife, would I have used it?

The driver chuckles as we get off the bus at the city gate. He seems to have enjoyed the incident. It's a relief to change buses.

We finally come to our stop. We walk along the highway, making no attempt to hide on back streets. No one speaks, but our pace quickens as we near the factory. Is Hawa right, that they'll let us back in?

The door is ajar. I go first, hoping with all my heart that I might see Hawa sitting at the desk waiting for us, that we might tell her what happened. Thank her. I will share my poem.

It's Ushi.

Once we've all filed in she gets up, shuts the door, locks it with a key that hangs from her belt, and returns to her chair. She looks at her watch, then at us. "It's seven," she says. "You are to go to work now and work through until your next shift, which of course starts at seven in the morning. For the inconvenience you've caused us . . ." She pauses. A half grin appears on her face. "You will receive points you'll never recover from." Her grin turns sour. "And you will not leave this factory again, unless a person in authority is accompanying you."

As if of one thought, we inch together until our bodies connect. We stand tall and strong and just look at her. We do not speak.

"Go!" she screams.

Thirty

WINTER HAS TAKEN its toll on us. We've become listless automatons, doing our jobs, eating, sleeping, thinking spring will never come, much less July and the promise of home.

Rumor spreads that the temperature today will be almost warm. I've been so numb with cold for the last four months that I believe it to be someone's joke. They gave us coats. I wear mine when I work, when I eat, and when I sleep. I pull it more tightly around me now. I can't imagine ever feeling warm again.

For the Chinese girls, standing in line here with us, warmer weather is great news. Today is a day off, and unlike those who are caged, they're free to leave and do whatever they want—which in most cases means looking for a better job. But what they're talking about are cherry blossoms. "There are five thousand cherry trees in the garden at Donghu Lake. That's where I'm going," someone says, and with her words the bars of the cage tighten around me till I have trouble breathing. How dare Ushi keep us locked in here when we can finally go out without worrying about frostbite? Crossing the highway and walking through the streets, penniless, while being whipped with ice-cold winds was not a pleasure we sought, but today . . .

I hold my bowl out for my ladle of breakfast mush, then trudge back to the room, choosing to sit alone on the bottom bunk. Mikray's.

I asked Jemile to be our emissary. Her sweetness prevails while the rest of us, especially me, have let anger creep into permanent position on our faces. We wanted to go to Donghu Lake in the Hubei Work Wear van with one of the little bosses. A small thank-you for surviving the winter and for carrying much of the workload while the Chinese girls dwindled in number, not willing to sacrifice their health, their lives, for a few yuan.

A day off? That's a real joke. Little bosses must have their day off, and Ushi is busy. Instead, perhaps as punishment for having had the audacity to ask, we're left at the factory to help the workmen. We push heavy carts, bring in bolts of blue denim and line them up against the wall. We oil the moving parts of the sewing machines. Bring in fresh shipping supplies. By some miracle we're not asked to clean the toilets.

And then we have a treat. Spy Girl shows up. The treat is the fact that she has to be here too and doesn't get the day off. Punishment for bad spying? She doesn't say. With two of the workmen at our side, probably brought along to ensure we don't run away, the door is opened and we're taken outside.

We're lined up two deep in front of the warehouse. Spy Girl holds a radio out in front of her. "You are to do eight minutes of calisthenics. Follow what it says," she tells us. There's a blast of pulsing music and then a female voice begins. "Arms above your head—two . . . three . . . four. Bring arms down—two . . . three . . . four. Right arm up and left arm down and stretch and two and three and four. Reverse arms. Left arm up and right arm down and stretch and two and three and . . ." The radio stops.

"Are you all so dumb you can't do what she says?" Spy Girl hollers.

Apparently. We have our Uyghur way of raising our arms, and it feels so good that perhaps we were carried away—remembering a dance, our own music. In fact, so good that I rip off my cheap, dirty, stinking coat and fling it to the ground, hoping to never, ever wear it again.

"Start again from the beginning," Spy Girl says through clenched teeth.

"Arms above your head—two, three, four . . ."

I try a little harder to pay attention. I stretch my arms to the sky, glide them up and down and around. I feel more alive than I have for some time.

"Arms to the side. Lunnnggge right and hold two, three, four. Lunnnggge left and hold two, three, four. Now squat and chant. Squat and chant with a ho-ha, ho-ha. Straight from the belly with a ho-ha, ho-ha."

We're ho-ha-ing with all our might and giggling and

laughing and crying. Quin Fong is screaming at us and we can't stop. It feels so good—ho-ha-ing, releasing our pent-up emotions into the fresh air.

"Get inside!" she shouts, but we don't move, and the workmen are laughing, not shoving us around. It's almost spring.

"Jemile," I say, pulling her next to me, "please ask if she'll let us try one more time—in your nicest, sweetest voice."

There's a twinkle in Jemile's eyes that I haven't seen before. She nods and goes with all her innocence and purity to stand in front of the ranting pale-purple-haired one.

"Please," Jemile says, reaching out but not touching. No one welcomes our touch. "Let us try one more time." When Quin Fong draws back, huffs in disdain, Jemile bows her head respectfully. "Perhaps," she continues, "if you were to lead us, to show us how to do the calisthenics, we would do much better." And I am so proud of her for thinking of this, because Spy Girl actually shrugs as if she'll consider it.

"Get back in line," she barks. "I didn't know how stupid you all were. Okay, if you can't follow the words, do what I do." She turns the radio back on and puts it on the ground. The music plays and we begin. I listen to the rhythm of the woman's voice and try hard not to watch Quin Fong, for she is far from graceful and I don't trust myself not to explode in laughter. This is the only fun we've had since we've been here; laughing would feel so good.

"That's better," Spy Girl says when the session ends. "We'll do it once again so you dummies can understand the importance of exercise to the well-being of our great nation."

My hands fly to my face to keep from smiling—from laughing out loud. It must be hard, being a spy for Ushi. Trying to be an Ushi or even a little boss. Quin Fong will never be promoted. I can only imagine that she's the daughter of some official Big Boss needs to have on his side. I'm delighted she's so inept and enjoys today's outdoor exercises as much as we do.

Thirty-One

TWO MORE WEEKS have passed, and I'm still cutting denim bib overalls with multiple reinforced tool and utility pockets, double knees that can accommodate kneepads, hammer loops and brush loops, and leg openings that fit over boots. Our time outside is a distant memory, but I complain less about the work now that we're finally getting paid. So many Chinese girls left the factory over the winter that Big Boss apparently decided that paying us would make us work harder and we'd happily do all the extra work. We were taken into Ushi's room to meet with the paymaster and each given two hundred and fifty yuan. It's a pathetic amount when you add up the hours we've worked, but it seems like a good sign. He didn't even mention points.

Big Boss has come around twice to give speeches about the importance of this work. Some company in Australia, a rush order. There will be a bonus if we finish before time. He doesn't say that his offer is only for the Chinese, so it might be for us too. We long ago decided that Big Boss and Ushi will have no interest in sending us back home when our time is up. We must be prepared to pay our own way. Every yuan they give us will go into pouches we sewed from stolen factory-floor material and carry tied around our waists—escape money for the journey home.

It's not Big Boss who visits today, it's Ushi who comes during our dinner break. When we finally removed our coats, they saw how skinny we'd all become and decided we might work better if given more time to eat and recover. We now have a half-hour break before returning to work.

"Line up," Ushi says, pointing to the hallway outside our room where she's standing. "Eat, and listen. The Australian company managers are coming tomorrow. You'll be let off an hour early tonight so you can wash your uniforms—and yourselves. If one of the managers asks you a question or tries to talk to you, you are *not* to answer. One person in each section has been chosen to be the contact. Only they will speak. Do you understand?" She looks at us, the Uyghur girls. Why would we break her rules? Not one of us wants points.

I spend the rest of the day and the next conjugating verbs and practicing sentences, having little conversations with myself in English. I know that's the language Australians speak, and focusing on English is a good distraction from the boredom of pockets and sleeves and hammer loops. I'm ashamed that I've let myself forget some important words. I want to be a master of at least three languages. I hope our visitors will say a few words in English so I can test my skills.

By midafternoon no visitors have come. Little Boss is exhausted from straightening our piles, from making us look efficient, wide-awake, and happy. We are happy workers, even if it takes a rod at our calves to make us so. The cutters are the first workers the visitors will see when they come onto the factory floor. We are to make a good impression.

It's hard to smile when they finally walk in. There are two men. The tough-looking one wears denim, not unlike what we're cutting, only his takes the form of tight-fitting blue jeans. His long-sleeved shirt is blue too, unbuttoned from the top so that it shows off his chest hair. His close-shaved head makes him look mean, as do his steely eyes, which sweep the room. The other man is fat and double-chinned. He wears an open-collared striped shirt that barely buttons over his big belly. The tough-looking one talks to Big Boss, who does his usual head nodding, half bowing.

The fat one interrupts them with a jerk of his head, and the entourage moves on, into sewing. Ushi looks nervous as she follows along. Handling important clients is definitely a job for Hawa, not Ushi. Again, I wonder where Hawa is. It's been months since anyone saw her, and we will not ask Ushi or Spy Girl about her. Chen disappeared soon after Zuwida's funeral. Our one Chinese friend. Gone. We don't know why.

When the group returns to cutting, I know there's trouble. The fat one's mouth is working to get out the few Mandarin words he seems to know. His hands are flying, pointing here and there, as he tries to put words to his displeasure. The mean one takes him by the arm and pulls him aside. With the back of his hand he lets Big Boss and Ushi know they're to stay where they are.

What they've come to look at are the stacks of material yet to be processed. The stacks are very close to where my cutting table is.

I bite my lips to keep from smiling, because they're speaking English.

"He never told us his factory was this small." The fat one's head is shaking, his jowls swinging back and forth. "His workers are already exhausted. Look at them. And he says he'll have them work overtime from now on. I bet they've been working overtime for weeks." He swivels around, startling me. "Have you?" he asks.

My mouth opens to say yes before I can swallow the word. Before I realize what I'm doing. What I've done! I've been standing here watching, listening. The scissors aren't even in my hand.

"I think we have our answer," he says, laughing. "I'm glad someone here speaks English and is willing to tell the truth."

If he's still looking at me, I'll never know. I'm pretending to cut a pocket—if only I could hold the scissors without shaking.

They keep talking—and I keep listening. Big Boss has too much of their money for them to back out now. "We made a big mistake, but we can't take it out on these poor girls. He'll work them until they die at their machines if we put more pressure on." I glance up. It's the mean-looking one who says this. Perhaps he's not so mean after all.

"Yeah, you're right," the fat one says. "But I'm not happy he's ruining our reputation. Let's go see what we can work out." They keep talking as they walk away. "After our shipment is delivered, we can make sure no one in Australia does business with this guy again."

I can't help but watch as they go back to where Big Boss and Ushi are standing. I have to see how they react to what the men say to them.

Ushi isn't watching the men walking toward her. She's watching me.

Thirty-Two

A LOUD WHIMPER ESCAPES from me as Little Boss thwacks my calves with her rod. It hurts, but I've learned not to cry out.

"What's going on with you? You're way behind," she says. "You think it's some kind of holiday because we have visitors?"

I don't bother to answer or even to look at her. Let Little Boss think what she will. It's Ushi I'm worried about. Maybe I'm imagining things, I tell myself. Ushi would have watched the men, not me.

Denim, bibs, pockets. Denim, bibs, pockets, I say over and over to myself, hoping to distract my mind. That doesn't work, so every few times I say it, I add another piece. I'm up to *denim, legs, bibs, pockets, loops. Denim, legs, bibs, pockets, loops* when a hand taps my shoulder.

"Ushi wants to see you." It's Quin Fong, whispering—spitting—into my ear. It's almost as if I expected this. I stop midcut. Follow.

I'm taken to Ushi's "interrogation room." As before, Ushi sits behind the table in her barren office.

She studies me. I study her. Her face shows no particular expression. My face is as expressionless as I can make it.

"So," she says after a long minute of staring, "you speak English."

"Yes, I do," I say.

"Good," she says. The metal frame of her chair scrapes against the concrete floor as she pushes it back. Stands. Tries to be taller than I am.

"You are going to dinner with Mr. Lee and the gentlemen from Australia. Quin Fong has clothes for you to wear. She'll try to make you attractive. You are to tell us every word of what they say in English." She glares at me for a few seconds. Then sits down. "Do you understand?"

I understand from stories I've heard that being chosen by the boss is the worst thing that can happen. Boss Lee can do anything he wants with me, and I'm being dressed in fancy clothes and going out with him. A bile mass churns in my stomach and explodes from my mouth and nose. I bend over. Gagging. Coughing.

"That's disgusting," Ushi says, and I hear the chair scrape again. "Clean her up the best you can, Quin Fong. She's going no matter what."

A door slams.

Slowly I raise my head. Look at the mess. It's not that bad. When so little goes into your stomach, there's not much to come out.

Spy Girl seems to be struggling not to vomit herself. Her face is pale. "We have to get a bucket. . . ." She stops. Wipes her hand over her mouth. "And clean it up." Now both hands are over her mouth, and she makes a quick exit.

I have to sit. I go to Ushi's chair. Collapse. My arms cushion my head as it drops to the table. I smell the stench of my vomit and hope some of it stays ingrained forever in the wood—for Ushi to smell every time she sits here.

Spy Girl returns and bangs the bucket on the floor. "Well, get over here. Start cleaning," she says.

The "we" has been forgotten. I alone am to scrub. And I do. This is not the battleground I choose. Quin Fong is not a worthy opponent.

Task done, I'm taken to a toilet room where I get to clean the bucket. Hanging in the same room, on a towel hook, are two "cute" outfits. I feel myself getting sick again.

"Take off your smock," Quin Fong says. "Let's see if either of these fits."

"No," I say.

"What makes you think you have a choice?" Spy Girl says, and for the first time I have some respect for her. It's hard for me to think of her as a victim, but maybe she is too, of something she doesn't quite understand but is forced to obey.

"I could call Ushi." She stops, gives a nervous little laugh. "Or Mr. Lee," she says, trying to make her voice sound high and mighty.

I want to laugh, but she's right. She could—and she would.

"Hand me the skirt," I say. "The black one." It's less offensive and maybe a bit longer than the fluorescent-green one. Still, when I pull it on under my smock it barely covers my underpants.

"The black blouse," I say, in my imperious voice. Maybe she won't notice that my hand is trembling when I take it from her.

I turn around, remove my smock, and quickly pull the blouse over my head. The deep-cut neck leaves the top of my breasts exposed and my arms totally bare, with only a little ruffle at the shoulder. *I can't do this!*

"You have to find me something else!" I scream. "I do not and will not ever wear this kind of thing! It's against the values of my people. We cover our arms, our legs . . . our hair . . ." My voice dies away because Spy Girl just shakes her head back and forth, stares at me as if she doesn't even hear.

"You don't wear a bra. You have no boobs—that means breasts. We've got to at least push you up a bit. I've got an extra bra," she says. "Stay here. I'll get it."

Quin Fong is embarrassed for me. She's trying to fix me up like they did Hawa. Will Spy Girl come back with a new name for me, too? I'm no Kitten. Maybe they'll call me Dog. And where *is* Hawa? Why isn't she going with the men? Doesn't she know English?

I'm in tears and clutching my jade necklace, because what will I do with it? I can't—I won't wear it! It's too sacred for these people to see. But where can I hide it?

Spy Girl comes back and I turn away from her again. Take off the blouse. Put on the bra. Put the blouse back on. Ahmat's jade piece is clutched in my hand as I turn to face her.

"Doesn't change much, does it," she says. "Okay. Let's keep going. Stockings." She hands me two long maroon lace things. I slip my necklace into the bra and fit the stockings over my feet, up my legs until they're above my knee-caps but below the skirt. Then shoes.

"No," I say. "I could never walk in those. I won't wear them."

Spy Girl looks at the two pairs she's holding out to me and shrugs. "You have to."

"No," I say again. "Give me the ones you're wearing now, and you wear those." I point to her lower-heeled sandals.

"Good idea," she says, and she actually takes the shoes off her feet and gives them to me. She seems to love the strappy ones I rejected. I guess I've done her a favor.

"Well, let's go see Ushi." She takes one more good look at me and rolls her eyes. "You're her problem, not mine."

I grab my smock and try to cover myself as I'm led back into Ushi's office.

She's sitting at her desk.

"Well, look what we have here." Ushi gets up. Circles around me, closer and closer, then grabs the smock and rips it out of my hands. "You won't need this, sweetheart," she says. Maybe that's my new name. Sweetheart.

It's as if I'm standing before her naked. How will this short skirt and scanty blouse help me to understand English, to do the job they want me to do? I'm reasonably pretty and I am tall and slender and graceful. Why is that not enough?

"Here's the story, sweetheart. The guys from Australia are unhappy, especially the, uh—" I think she wants to say *the short, fat one*, but that would be describing herself and she can't seem to do it. "The, uh . . . white-haired one. He's the guy with the money. You"—and now she's right in my face—"you are going to make him . . . happy. Tell him he's cute, get him drunk, whatever you have to do to get him to talk. He doesn't seem to know much Mandarin, so that's why you're here. He's planning something. But he still owes us money, and we want it before he pulls any tricks. Do you understand?"

Only too well, but I don't say that. There is no way I'll tell him he's cute or try to get him drunk.

"I ask you, do you understand!" She's shouting now as she pulls my arms away from my body, where they've been glued in my pathetic attempt to cover myself.

"You want me to spy," I say quietly.

She snorts. "Yeah, like that," she says. "If you only knew, sweetheart. If you only knew." She looks at her watch. "We still have some time. Quin Fong, get your makeup. Do her face. Do whatever you can. And you," she says, pointing to me. "Sit."

Quin Fong must have been ready for her assignment.

She goes to the toilet room and returns with a bag. Empties it onto the table.

Ushi keeps watch. I sit stiff and unmoving. *I can wash it all off when I get where I'm going,* I keep saying to myself.

"I like the paleness of her skin tone," Spy Girl says. "I'll just give her some rouge."

A brush hits my cheek. Quin Fong steps back, takes a look, does the other side. "It's the eyes that need the most work," she says. "Purple shadow. That's good." And she keeps talking as she stabs at my eyes with a black pencil and then goes after my eyebrows. She pulls something from a tube and starts attacking my eyelashes until they're so thick with paint or something that I can hardly move my eyelids.

She stands back and takes a look. "How's that?" she asks Ushi.

"An improvement," Ushi says. "She's beginning to look the part. Do something with her lips now. You know, big and pouty. And then her hair."

Spy Girl puts lipstick on me that tastes like berries. It's not the taste that repulses me, it's knowing that the color of raspberries is now slashed across my lips. Then she pulls my hair to one side, pins it, and drapes it over my shoulder.

"Show her what she looks like now," Ushi says. "It'll help her play her part."

"No thank you," I say. "I have no desire to see myself."

"Doesn't matter, sweetheart. Everyone else can."

She looks at her watch again. "Good job, Quin Fong.

This is one thing you do very well. So," she says, turning to me, "it's time to go downstairs. The car should be here to pick you up."

I can't move. I don't know what my options are—no, I'm aware I have none—but my body doesn't respond.

Ushi takes my arm in a bruising grip and jerks me to my feet. "Oh no," she says. "Those can't be the shoes you're wearing! Well, it's too late now. Anyway, no one is going to be looking at your feet." She marches me to the door and down the stairs.

A fancy black car is waiting outside the factory. Big Boss is driving. He gives Ushi a nod. She opens the door to the back seat and shoves me in.

Thirty-Three

I'M IN THE BACK SEAT. Alone. Boss Lee doesn't say anything, just drives like a maniac, careening around cars, buses, people. Headlights blind me. Horn blasts pierce my ears. I try to pay attention. It seems important to know where I'm being taken. We're on the highway, headed east. Small towns, cities emerge in the darkness. He keeps driving.

Now there are higher buildings on both sides. Nothing but city in every direction. A city engulfed in garish neon signs—beside us, in the sky. Whole buildings of gold. Some orange. Or blue and red. And Big Boss keeps turning right, then left, through so many streets I lose track. And people. Lots of people. *Help me. Please,* I plead silently.

I don't need to be afraid, do I? I'm here because I speak English. The men are nice. They worried about us working overtime. I'm Ushi's spy, not a painted woman.

Big Boss jams on the brakes and stops in front of a hotel. "You're to report to me every word they say in English. Got it? Every word," he repeats. He turns, looks at me. "And you are to give them whatever they want." He narrows his eyes. "Whatever they ask for." He cocks his head.

"The one with the belly likes girls who speak English. You got that, honey?"

I sink back into the seat. My head shakes back and forth.

Slowly I let my hand go to my face. I touch my glossy lips. My fingers go to my eyelashes. The stuff they're encrusted with leaves a black stain on my fingertip.

My hand falls to my lap. I *am* painted.

The car door opens. The fat one gets into the back seat. "Hi, honey," he says.

My name is now Honey.

My breath comes in desperate gasps. I have to choose. Fierce or arrogant? Mikray or Hawa? I'm neither. I crouch against the door.

"Ah, come on, honey," he says. "All I want is to hear a little English. You look so cute tonight."

Big Boss clears his throat. He can't know what the man said, but he knows I didn't answer.

I mumble, "Hello."

The tall one sits in front. Doors close. We speed into the streets. "We're ten minutes from my club," Big Boss says, and then goes into a speech about the great city, pointing out the amazing sights.

The tall one leans over the seat back to talk to the fat one. "Why did we agree to come?" he says in English.

"We're here. Might as well make him pay for our booze and good time. Right?"

Big Boss clears his throat again.

We stop in front of a plain-looking building. Big Boss gets out. Hands some money to a uniformed man standing out front, then opens my door. He grabs my elbow. Pulls me out. And doesn't let go. I walk with him and the two men to the door of the club as the car is driven away. Another man in uniform opens the club door.

There's an explosion of noise and flashing lights. I'm dragged into a huge room of throbbing beats. Streaks of red, blue, green burst before my eyes. I see almost-naked dancers on a stage, throwing their arms and legs around. Men reach out and touch them, and they don't seem to mind.

"How do you like this, guys?" Big Boss calls out. "Pretty good, huh?"

"Yeah, good," the fat one says, loosening his tie. He, the tall one, and Boss are all wearing suits and ties. "Let's get a drink."

"Follow me," Boss says. "I've reserved a table."

His grip still firm on my arm, he pulls me through the crowd of gyrating bodies—dancing, singing, drinking, hollering to one another. We go through an open arch into a room off to the side. Lots of people, but it's quieter. The ceiling is flooded with lavender light. The red and blue glass walls give off a muted glow above the long fuchsia couch that snakes around the oval room. A hostess greets Big Boss, and we walk on a plush carpet to a low table with lights under the glass top. The tall one, the fat one, and I sit on the couch, in that order. Boss sits on a special seat across the table so he can face all of us. He gives the hostess some money. She smiles and leaves. Other girls come over. They're all Chinese, wearing nice blouses and skirts. They want to know what the men would like to drink. When I'm asked, I shake my head. Boss orders something for me, I don't know what.

They return with our drinks and some food. And stay and talk. Each man has a special girl. One wiggles her way in between the Australian men. One is next to the tall one. And one brings a stool over beside Big Boss. They laugh and giggle, flip their hair, say cute things.

I finally take a deep breath. Maybe everything will be all right after all. I eat some fruit they have brought to the table. It is delicious.

Then the fat one takes my hand in his. "Talk to me, honey. I'm bored. I don't understand a word they're saying."

I freeze, and he knows it. "Now don't be afraid, little honey. I'm not going to hurt you."

"I . . . I can translate for you. Let me try. It could be fun," I say. And for a while I do, and it's a game. His girl speaks no English, so I can say most anything I want and deceive them both.

All the voices get louder and louder. The men have long ago taken off their jackets, loosened their ties. The talk is all silly nonsense. The girl near Big Boss keeps ordering drinks. Yet another round is brought in. I still haven't touched mine. She takes it. Leaves another. "It's water," she whispers, and slips a paper under my thigh.

"I'm thirsty. I need to drink," I say to the fat one. "You pay attention to your girl for a while. Okay?" My words are all sugar, and I hate myself for the sound of my voice, but he does what I tell him and I lift my glass, hoping I'll have a chance to read the note. The water trickles down my throat. Then I gulp it. I'm so thirsty. No one seems to notice. Big Boss is paying attention to the girl beside him. I unfold the note. Glance down. The note is in Uyghur. *Go to the ladies' room. We need to talk. Hawa.*

My body begins to tremble. I can't stop it. Somehow I get the words out. "I have to go to the ladies' room."

"Can't handle your drinks, can you, honey? That's all right, you'll be more fun," the fat one says, laughing.

The drink girl is beside me, helping me stand, leading me to the ladies' room. I open the door, and there is Hawa in a white blouse and black skirt. Tall, stately, beautiful even under her thick layer of makeup. There is no past that can keep us from clinging to each other.

"Hawa," I say after we let go. "You . . . here . . . We didn't know."

"I never came back after I was taken here to entertain Mr. Lee's clients. They drugged me, Roshen. Forced a man on me." Her eyes close as she turns away. "I couldn't go back."

"But . . . Zuwida? You left the package for us when she died."

"Mikray's friend is a good man. He let me know. He took her to the hospital, helped me arrange for the burial. You were brave to go."

Hawa starts pushing me toward the door. "You must not be gone too long. Mr. Lee will notice. Here's what we'll do."

"But . . . everything's all right, isn't it? They each have a girl."

Hawa looks at me. "How did you get here, Roshen?"

I can't return her gaze. I search the floor. "I made a mistake," I say. "Ushi found out I speak English. They're Australian. I'm supposed to report what they say."

"The white-haired one wants you. You're tall, you're a virgin. He likes that."

"He *has* a girl," I say.

Hawa shakes her head. "The other man will take both Chinese girls. Mr. Lee has already paid for them."

No one else is in the room, but we move away from the entrance. "What's happening is real. Listen carefully," she says. "Keep calling for drinks. Get him drunk. I'll be watching."

"But, Hawa, you're working."

"Not tonight. Tonight I'm keeping you safe. Never, ever let Mr. Lee bring you back to the club—no matter what! Do not take pills or drinks that they give you. Do you understand?" She takes my hands in hers. "Don't let this happen to you," she says.

"Oh, Hawa. I'm so sorry," I say, and squeeze her hands. I don't want to let go.

She shakes me away. "Pretend. Be coy. Tell him you don't want him to touch you because you're shy. When Mr. Lee goes off with his girl, he'll make sure you go off with the white-haired one. Get him to the room. I'll know where you're going. I'll be in the toilet room. There'll be a special drink waiting for him. Get him into bed. Take his pants off if he wants you to. He'll try to undress you, but say you'll do it yourself in the toilet room and surprise him. Turn the lights out and leave no more than one candle burning. He won't know I'm the one who comes back into the room." She starts walking toward the door.

"He'll probably fall asleep," she says. "When the phone rings, his time is up. Get him downstairs. He's gotten what he wants. He'll be harmless."

"Hawa . . ." I try to find words. Nothing comes out, but my arms encircle her. I hold her close.

"There's no good escape from the factory, Roshen," she whispers. "But you have to do something while you're still pure. They'll force you to come again. Don't be stained by their ugliness."

Thirty-Four

AT THE QURBAN Heyit—the Feast of the Sacrifice—
Uyghurs celebrate the story of Abraham, who was willing to sacrifice his child according to God's command.
Abraham was released from this command and allowed to
substitute a lamb for his son. Is God asking that I be sacri-
ficed? I do not submit by my own free will. And is my sister
Hawa to be offered in my place?

I stand in the doorway longer than I intend. The
girl who led me to the ladies' room again takes my arm.
Seats me. Places a drink in front of me, whispering "water" as she bends her head. She passes drinks to everyone.

The double-chinned one's arm goes around me. His
other arm is on my knee, rubbing my net stocking. The
arm to get rid of first is the one on my knee. I grab his hand
before it gets farther up. "You have to leave one arm free
if you're going to keep drinking," I say in what I think is a
cute, friendly voice. I guide his hand to his drink. Help him
pick it up. Guide it to his mouth. "That's better," I say as I
slip forward, out from under the sweaty arm he's thrown
over my shoulders.

"So, what happened while I was away? Did you get

lonely?" I ask. He lunges toward me, tries to nestle his big head on my shoulder. I said the wrong thing.

"No, no. Not here," I find myself saying. "We can do that later." I'm all bubbly or hysterical, maybe both.

"Ahh, honey. You are an innocent, aren't you. So sweet," he says, pecking my cheek.

"Why don't you tell me about Australia and what you do there. I'd love to know." Apparently that's the right thing to say, and he drinks and talks. I guess the promise of later was all he needed. I make sure he isn't watching Big Boss or his friend, whose girls climb all over them, sit on their laps, make sure the men drink a lot. I think it might go on forever. And then it doesn't.

Big Boss calls the hostess over. She escorts the tall one and his two girls from the room and returns too quickly. Smiles at the fat one. Helps him up. He's wobbly. She takes his arm. Steadies him. She gives me a quick nod and I follow. We go down a long hallway with doors to many rooms on both sides. She opens a door.

"This is nice," the man says, looking into the softly lit room with its large bed. He grabs the hand of the hostess and begins to pull her in. She untangles herself and places my hand in his.

I can't bring myself to cross the threshold. What if there's a mistake? What if Hawa isn't hiding in this room? My chest heaves as I yank my hand free. I turn to the hostess but she's disappeared.

An iron hand grips my arm. The fat one is not that

drunk. "Don't play innocent, honey," he says. "Your boss owes me—bigtime—and he said you were more than willing to help him out by offering me something quite special this evening to make up for it. Right?" He smiles.

My strength drains from me. I can't overpower this man. If it's the wrong room—if Hawa isn't here—I'll kill him, somehow. Then I'll be killed. Or rot in prison.

He drags me toward the bed.

Pretend! That's what Hawa said to do. Pretend.

"You—you don't understand," I stammer. "I'm shy. I want you to be gentle . . . and kind." My words are meant to be coy and cute, but I sound like a schoolgirl begging the teacher not to use a whip.

He loosens his hold.

"You're right," I say, my voice more under control. "Let's go to the bed so you can get comfortable."

"Yeah, honey. That's a fine idea."

I take hold of him now, the way the hostess did, and lead him to the edge of the bed. "You sit here and I'll take off your shoes. That should feel good." He's grinning as I kneel in front of him and remove his shoes. He's also got his fingers in my hair, following it down over my shoulders, stroking it. Stroking my breast. I move away. Leave his socks on.

"Lie down now," I tell him as soon as I can breathe again—convince myself not to kill him. "I'll lower the lights for us."

"Don't turn them all off," he says. "I want to see you."

"You will," I say, "but candlelight will make it very romantic. Don't you think?"

He makes a low, rumbling sound and leans back against the pillows. What I'm doing is working, so far. My body trembles as I move about, but I'm managing.

There's a tray of drinks by the candle I leave burning. One of the drinks is set apart, and I know that's the one I am to give him. I still don't know if Hawa is here, but this is a hopeful sign.

"Why don't we have a little drink and then I'll loosen your shirt collar. It looks too tight and uncomfortable." I'm already standing over him with the drink. He reaches for it. I pull it away.

"Wait a minute," I say in a sickening, gooey voice. "Let me help you." He has to drink it! Even if I have to pour it down his throat.

He seems to like it—or he likes that I'm touching his head, lifting it up so that not one drop is spilled. I still hold his head while I put the glass down, smooth a pillow, and push him down. I unbutton his shirt, releasing his double chins.

Now I don't know what to do, but he does. "Let's see how that blouse of yours comes off, shall we, honey?" And he's touching me again, mauling me. I get away. Stand up.

I know it's too soon for me to go to the toilet room. He's not yawning or looking tired enough. I remember Hawa's words. *His pants if you have to.*

"Let's get your pants off first," I say, not having any

idea how I'm going to go about it. "You would like that, wouldn't you?" He's nodding like a fool.

"I'm going to help, but you have to promise to keep your hands off me." I sound like a schoolteacher. I can't find any more sweet words.

"Okay, honey," he says, and chuckles. "I'll try." I guess he thinks we're playing a game.

I unbuckle his belt. Undo the button. He starts struggling with the zipper himself, with an urgency I don't like. But his movements are clumsy, faltering.

"That's enough for now, don't you think? Lie back on the pillow for a minute. Rest. We have lots of time."

"Let's get you undressed. I want to see that beautiful body of yours." His eyelids are fluttering, but he grabs the ruffle on my blouse.

This time I take his arms and fold them across his chest.

"You know what I am going to do for you?" As abhorrent as it is to me, I bend close to him, take his big head in my hands, and rock it back and forth. "I am going into that room over there and taking off all of my clothes. Then I am coming back with a surprise. Will that be all right?"

"Great, honey. Do it quick." His words slur a little, but he's awake.

I wait a few more seconds, until my heart is pounding so desperately I'm afraid he'll notice. I don't know what I'll do if Hawa isn't there, but I can't let any more time pass.

"Hurry," he says. "I've got a real hard-on for you."

Thirty-Five

No one is in the toilet room when I open the door. "Hawa?" I whisper.

She steps out from behind the shower curtain. "I had to make sure it wasn't he who came," she says.

I stand motionless, tears streaming down my face. I can't believe we have to go through with Big Boss's promise.

"Leave the door slightly open so we can hear him," Hawa tells me.

She still has her clothes on.

"I told him . . . I told him I'd come back naked," I say.

"All right," she says. "Did you find the drink?"

I nod. "He drank all of it."

"Good," she says. "The room seems dark enough."

I nod again. "Just one candle. I got all the lights out. Hawa, I . . ."

She puts her finger to my lips.

"We'll talk after. He'll probably sleep for a while."

Then Hawa removes her clothes and walks out into the room. I close the bathroom door to a crack.

"Close your eyes," she says to him in Mandarin. "I'll tell you when to open them again."

"Honey, none of that foreign stuff." He drawls his words. "Talk to me in English."

Hawa says nothing.

He'll know it isn't me! I sink to the floor. Helpless. Both of us caught in our deception.

It's quiet. Too quiet.

Then I hear moans and grunts from the fat one. Squeals of pain from Hawa that sound so fake I almost laugh. And in the sweetest voice, Hawa lets out a stream of vulgar Uyghur words, calling him every lowly animal that crawls upon this earth.

Then it is quiet again.

Hawa comes back. Showers. Dresses. Comes to me. "You're a mess," she says, and hands me a wet cloth. My flood of tears has not cleansed my painted face. Nor can it wash away the shame that has fallen on both of us.

Even so, I rub my face until I think the skin might come off. Most of the eye stuff and rouge and lipstick are now on the cloth.

Hawa squats beside me on the floor. I turn to her. "Why, Hawa?" I say. "Why are you doing this? I hate Boss Lee!"

"Yes. He's pathetic. What he's done to you is evil. My path is not a good one, but yours is different."

She rises quickly. Glances into the room. "He's still sleeping." She comes back to me, checks her watch. "There are things I want you to know." Her eyes send the same message that was on her face when she was first named

Kitten and left our room—determination, strength, and fear. She does not hold my gaze. She turns away. "It seems important that someone know what happened."

I barely hear her at first. Her voice is hollow, far away. "My father was a successful trader. He needed support from the new Chinese cadre to keep doing business. Putting my name on the cadre's list to be sent south was the deal they arranged, but my father would do it only if the cadre agreed to get me special training. I didn't mind. I was arrogant and willful like my father," Hawa says, her voice more animated now. "I thought I was special and could become a successful businesswoman, but it wouldn't happen if I stayed in Hotan. I agreed to come; Mr. Lee was to train me." Her words become hurried as she keeps glancing at her watch. The fat one's time must almost be up.

"When I was finally brought down to Mr. Lee's office, he saw what I could do. I was much more useful and clever than Ushi. I went on business calls with him. Then the businessmen came to the factory. For the first time, he asked me to go to the club to help him. But he got too busy with his own whore to pay attention to me. The men drugged me and raped me." She gives a violent shake to her body. "Ushi planned it. I know she did. She hated me. Loved the thought of my being raped.

"I couldn't go back to the factory. There was nothing for me there anymore. I'd learned all I could from Mr. Lee, and I couldn't be around Ushi. I asked Mr. Lee to arrange for me to work at his club. He had the cadre tell my family that I was on the path of my new career." Her body jerks with silent laughter.

For a moment the imperious Hawa I remember so well returns. "I let myself get into this. I'll get myself out. I've made a lot of money," she says. "Soon I'll escape across the southern border and be free. I'll do it, Roshen. I'll be as successful a businessperson as that fat man lying out there."

"But your home? Your family?"

"The purity of my body and spirit is gone forever. I will never be welcomed home. No one back there will want me." She takes my hands in hers. "I have your notebook, Roshen. The factory boy brought it to me. It was in our language; he thought it might be valuable. May I keep it with me? Your own poems, the ones you wrote, give me courage and comfort."

My hands cover my mouth to keep me from crying out. "Yes. Oh, Hawa. Yes." I grasp her. Hug her to me. "May Allah be with you."

She tears herself away. "It's time," she says. Her face becomes fierce. "You must leave the factory. You have to. Do you hear me? I may not be here next time. I hope I'm not. I'll be all right, but you must take care of yourself. Do you understand?"

Then she's gone.

I wait for the phone call. I think I should be getting him up and dressed, but I can't face what might happen —that he might touch me again.

Then the phone rings and I must go to him. "Time is

up," I say. "Time to go back to the party." I think that's a good thing to say. "You can get dressed by yourself, can't you?" Even in the dim light I see his nakedness, his private parts hanging out of his unzipped pants. I look away. I hate seeing this. Bile stirs in my stomach. If he says he needs my help, I'll zip his pants up and squeeze him until he howls like an animal.

He's just taken my virginity. He can't expect anything more. "I . . . I'm a bit shaken right now. I hurt a little," I say, hating the sound of my voice. I want to let out a string of Uyghur curses and condemn him to eternal life in hell.

"Honey, come over here. Let me give you a little hug. You're so sweet."

"They're expecting us downstairs." I head for the door. "I'll go tell them you're on your way."

"No, honey. Give me a minute here," he says, struggling to get up. He pulls his pants up and closes the zipper. He puts his shirt on, buttons it enough to cover his belly, tucks it in. He picks up his jacket and tie and heads toward me. I rush out the door into the hallway. I'll scream if he touches me.

The hostess greets us when we return to the lounge. Big Boss and the tall one are already there, and the girls. More drinks are brought in. The fat one seems content to sit for a while. Then he leans toward me. "What were you saying to me up there?" He looks puzzled. "I didn't understand a word of it."

"It was Uyghur," I say. "My native language. I forgot

my English for a moment." My voice is cold and stony as I say this.

He shrugs. Goes back to sitting in his stupor, then begins to yawn.

Big Boss keeps looking over. He's now more interested in the fat one than in his girl. He should be. The fat one has the money. "It's been a long evening," Boss says. "Maybe it's time to leave."

"Mr. Lee is asking if you'd like to go back to the hotel," I translate.

"Tell him I am tired. Very happy, honey." He stops talking. Grins. "But ready to go."

"He'd like to leave," I say.

The tall one is still having a good time. He'll stay. Boss, the fat one, and I make our way through the crowds, the noise, the flashing lights, into the street. The car is waiting for us. As much as I abhor touching the fat one, I grab him by the elbow and escort him to the front seat. Stuff him in and shut the door. The attendant looks surprised that I took over his job but says nothing. He opens the back door. I slide in.

Boss Lee is full of effusive words of appreciation for the fat man's understanding, and I translate in even more flattering terms. Boss guarantees that the next deadline will be met, and I say only that every effort will be made to meet the date.

We're about to pull up in front of the hotel when a hand creeps over the front seat. It's filled with yuan notes.

He flutters them, trying to get my attention, I guess. I turn away. He leans over the seat, clears his throat. "Honey?" he says. I'm as far away as I can get—looking out the window. "Hon-ey?" he says again.

He throws the money. It scatters on the seat. On the floor.

Boss Lee sees this. He jumps out of the car. Goes to the other side to help the doorman extract the fat one from the car and walks with him to the hotel door, uttering useless Mandarin words of apology for my rude behavior. The double-chinned, fat-bellied one waves him away. He's had what he wants. He's paid for it. He's ready for bed.

Boss gets back into the car. Slams the door. The car motor roars as he takes off. "You're an ignorant peasant!" he screams. "You insulted him! If you just ruined this deal for me, I'll make you pay bigtime." Then he roars his engine some more as we careen through the streets.

We are the tamarisk.
Pink white flowers our deception,
For we are barren in this foreign soil,
Our roots deep planted in the desert sand.

Will these words I once wrote and put in my notebook give me the courage and comfort I need now, as they once helped Hawa?

The ride back to the factory seems shorter than the ride to the club. Drunken Boss believes he's invincible, and we arrive safely only because of the careful driving of others who know to get out of the way of this speeding madman. The factory is dark. Shut down for the night. I jump out, run to the door, and am surprised to find it unlocked. I don't look back to see what Boss is doing. I dash up the stairs. No Ushi, no Spy Girl.

One dim light is left on in the toilet room. I go to a dark corner. I step out of the shoes, rip the maroon stockings from my legs and throw them in the garbage. I rip off the ruffly blouse and throw it in the garbage. Next the skirt, my panties.

The bra.

I am left with only the white jade necklace.

I am no longer worthy of the purity I hold in my hands. It has been touched by an unclean man. A pig. I place it underneath the clothing to be buried with the trash, deep in the earth from which it came.

Perhaps someday it will be found and hang again on the breast of a pure soul.

I creep, naked, along the shadow of the walls and go to bed.

Thirty-Six

THE ROOM FILLS with hushed voices as I climb down from my bunk the next morning. "We were worried, Roshen," Adile says, coming to my side. "Are you all right?"

No is the real answer, but not the one I give. "I made a mistake," I say, and I don't recognize my voice. My head spins. I grab the bed pole and sit.

A hand strokes mine. "It's all right, Roshen," a voice says, and I know it is Jemile. Jemile. I told her it was all right that a man touched her breast and under her panties —the man tried to hurt her and she escaped, I said. But it's *not* all right. She was tainted—ruined by the touching. Jemile will never be the same. Nor will I.

Long-overdue tears flow from my eyes as I look at my Uyghur sisters huddled around me.

For the moment I feel safe. I wipe my face with the backs of my hands. "Ushi found out I speak English. I was forced to go to Boss Lee's club with him to translate for one of the visitors." I stop. It's hard to get the words out. There is much I'll never tell them. "It . . . it was awful. Noisy, lots of drinking, dancing. They made me dress like Quin Fong and wear makeup." I lean against the pole, signal that I have no more to say.

"We worked late," Adile says. "You weren't here when we came upstairs. All we knew was that someone put your work smock on your bed. We're so glad to see you. You must have had little sleep."

"I'm glad to be back . . . and I'll be fine. We need to hurry or we'll be late," I say, and then I don't move.

In time I change into my work smock and join the exodus to the factory floor.

I like having sharp scissors in my hand. If only I'd had them with me. But where would I have hidden scissors in lace stockings and scanty, skintight clothing? It's too late for revenge against the fat one. I wish now for some disaster that would ruin Boss Lee, his factory, and every pair of overalls within its walls.

It's unsettling to let my mind stray from cutting denim. I try to lull my brain with mindless routine, but my thoughts drift to how I might sabotage the pieces I'm working on so the fat man's reputation is ruined. It's hard to make overall bibs and hammer loops lethal.

Then, the inevitable. Little Boss tells me to report to Ushi—at once.

I finish the pile of utility pockets I'm working on. Leave the scissors at my workstation and walk into the hallway. I regret I have not spent more time thinking about what part of the Australian men's conversations I'll tell.

"Sit," Ushi commands the minute I step into the room.

The chair faces her desk. I do not wish to look at her. I angle it toward the wall. I sit.

Ushi does not speak.

I set my face, my body, in stone so she can't know what I'm thinking. If she wants me to break down, to beg for help so she'll have me in her power and become a tool to her ambitions, I'll give her no satisfaction.

Ushi can't sit still. I can. I hear the rustle of paper. Little scrapes of metal chair legs on concrete floor. Then one giant scrape as she storms across the room and pounds on the door. "Mr. Lee, she's here," she says.

Boss Lee circles the desk and finally sits on the edge of it. "The Australian men spoke a lot of English yesterday. I want to know everything they said about me, about the factory." His voice is haughty, condescending.

I don't wish to answer. My voice has turned to stone too.

"Get the rod, Ushi. This one is stupid. She doesn't know what's good for her."

Ushi hits my legs from the side. One side. The other. Then directly on the front. I'm afraid she'll break my knee-caps.

"They said you lied to them." I speak, rather than take the chance of not being able to walk. "Your factory is so small you could never finish their job on time. And if they forced you, your workers would drop dead because they already look exhausted and must be working overtime."

"That's not true!" Boss shouts. He jumps up, stomps around until he ends up staring into my face. "What else? What else did they say?"

"If they were going to let you get away with it, they might as well enjoy a night on the town and have you pay for it."

Boss's eyes flare. "You're making that up." His fists tighten. I think he might hit me.

"No," I say in a clear, icy voice, looking right at him. "Why would I make it up when I know it will make you angry and you will probably hit me?"

If he was going to, he stops himself. Gnashes his teeth. "What else?"

"The overweight one said he was wealthy. He owns many enterprises. Would you like me to name them?"

His fists tighten again. I glare at him. His hands release. "There must be something else," he says.

"No, they were quite boring," I answer.

"Oh, boring, were they? I thought you had a good time, honey."

It takes me a second to understand what he's saying.

I get up and walk from the room.

"Come back here!" Ushi yells.

"No. Let her go," I hear Big Boss say.

Boss's words haunt me. Not a good spy, but good for other things, isn't that what he really meant? How long before I'm asked to "entertain" again? Customers are always intrigued by us Uyghur girls. They stop and point. Want to know about us. Am I a little something special for Boss to offer?

Later that night, before we fall into our beds, I gather

everyone as far from the door as possible. "I can't ever go out with Big Boss again," I say, and my body trembles. The fat man's stinking breath engulfs me again as Boss's words assault my ears: *I thought you had a good time, honey.*

I can't go on. Jemile takes my hands, strokes them gently. She's comforting me, when I should be comforting her! Warning her. Warning everyone. This isn't just about me, it's about all of us. "I'm not certain what we can do to defy Big Boss," I say. "I thought he wanted me to go because of my English . . . but he wanted . . . more." The words choke me. I hang my head. Am I more concerned with saving my saintly image than helping my sisters? *Wake up! Wake up! Wake up!* resounds in my head as words from this poem rush before my eyes:

> *The day will come, you will be so sorry,*
> *Then, you will understand the real meaning of my words.*
> *You will say "Oh," but it will be late.*
> *Then, Uyghur, you will think about my calls.*

I open my eyes. Study the girls surrounding me with new urgency. "Big Boss wanted me to spy for him," I say. "He also offered the fat man my virginity to help compensate for late delivery." Their hands fly to cover their mouths. Looks of horror cross their faces. "I was saved by an act of unbelievable compassion. . . ." Tears shroud my eyes, but I keep talking. "A brave and wonderful girl helped to get him drunk. She took my place, and he didn't know the difference. Big Boss thinks I 'had a good time' because the fat man was happy." I'm talking too fast now, but I can't slow down. "I'm certain he'll want me to please other clients," I say. "He may ask you. The girls he buys at the club are expensive. He doesn't have to pay us."

"He can't do this," Adile says too loudly.

I hope this isn't a night when Ushi patrols the hallway.

"They can do anything they want," I say. My voice is flat and hard. "I plan to become as repulsively ugly and dirty as I can. No hair washing or combing. No clean clothes. I'll lose more weight. I'll do everything I can think of. I apologize in advance for becoming a foul-smelling mess."

"Should we do that too?" Jemile asks.

"I don't think so, not yet. If they try to get you to go to the club with Big Boss, remind them how important you are to getting the job done on time. If you don't get your sleep, you won't be able to work. Do something disgusting while you say this, like picking your nose, anything so that a client wouldn't want you.

"If we can last for three and a half more months, we can go home."

Thirty-Seven

YOU CAN'T DO this, Roshen," Adile says. "You can't go without food. You're too thin already. You'll get sick."

"Nurse Adile, I'll be fine. To go with Boss Lee to the nightclub is worse than starving to death." Adile and I sit side by side on Mikray's bunk. She's spooning noodles into her mouth, while I'm trying to convince myself I'm not hungry.

"It will be all right if I miss a few more meals," I say. "Being unkempt may not be enough. Ushi could scrub me clean in the shower downstairs. Then I'd have two choices —do what Boss Lee wants or escape. You know only too well that there is no escape." I twist away in anger. "I could hide out until I'm caught and sent away for reeducation, or cross a border and exile myself forever from my home and all I hold dear. I'm not willing to do either."

Adile is laughing. "You won't have to do that, Roshen. You're quite unattractive already with your soiled clothes and your stink. But please don't starve yourself anymore. All I see are your hollow cheeks and bones," she says, and she is no longer laughing.

"I'm in control. I drink just enough so I can keep working." I tell her not to worry, though doubts about the success of my campaign haunt me daily. "Adile," I say, "if for any reason I do have to leave, will you make sure everyone gets home, that they save enough money?"

"I already have a job, and that's to keep you healthy. You're the one we need, the one who holds us all together. You know that, Roshen, don't you? It was your poems, the stories you told us during the long, cold winter months, that helped us survive. You gave us hope that we would return to our homes in East Turkestan, that our lives would, one day, be given back to us." By now many of the girls stand in front of my bunk listening to Adile, nodding as they scoop food into their mouths.

"I'm getting your bowl, Roshen," Adile says. "Then I'm taking you to the kitchen to get lunch. The noodles are almost edible today."

———

I try to follow Adile's advice. I fill my bowl with food, but I can't eat it. The taste is repulsive to me now, it turns my stomach. I pretend to eat, then throw it away. I get thinner every day. Weak, too, which bothers me. It's not a good feeling, and I'm having trouble working long hours. I know the sting of the rod too well. Too bad most of the bruises are under my smock—they would make me look even more ugly.

Today, however, I must be especially unattractive. Ushi notified us that important visitors are coming. Uniforms clean; we are not to speak.

It's a torturously long day, waiting for them. Little Boss probes and scolds. The customers come. They're speaking English. After much gesturing and bowing and scraping, Big Boss leads one of them toward my table. He passes me by—turns, takes another look, and is obviously repulsed by the gaunt, unappealing person he sees. He leads the man away with more gesturing and bowing.

I take a deep breath. It worked! I will not have to be Honey tonight. I can be the dirty, ignorant Uyghur girl he already thinks I am. Now I can eat. It's been a while since I had any food. But I don't feel hungry anymore, just dizzy. My head aches.

I hear the clack of footsteps coming my way. Little Boss. I place the pattern and start cutting, but I can barely open and close the scissors. They're so heavy.

The rod hits my calves and I . . . begin . . . to crumble.

Thirty-Eight

IT'S MORNING WHEN I wake. Gulnar holds my head. Adile spoons water into my mouth, her hand stroking my throat to help me swallow. I'm in Mikray's bunk.

"You fainted yesterday. They brought you upstairs," Adile says. "You must stay here and rest."

"No . . ." I try to sit up. My head swoons. I fall back. They're right, I can't work today.

"We have to go," Adile says. "We left water and food. Drink and eat all you can."

"Please, do it for us," Gulnar says. "We need you."

Then they're gone. And I do, I try. I spill the water, but some goes into my body. I eat a spoonful of porridge. I think Big Boss will not try to use me again. Now I must get strong so I can work. I'm certain I'll need the money for my return trip home.

Another sip of water is all I manage before sinking onto the bed. I'll go back to work at noon, I tell myself.

———

I hear the stampede of girls running upstairs. It's the noon break. I try to sit up. It is not so bad this time. Adile rushes in. Gives me a gentle hug. "I'll bring more water and food," she says. Jemile sits next to me when Adile leaves. She takes my hand. I think they've decided not to leave me alone, and I love their comfort. It gives me strength.

Lunchtime is short. I sip more water. Try to eat a spoonful of soup. I'm still wearing my smock—they put me in the bed with it on, and I've not had the energy to remove it. With help, I stand. I'm wobbly at first. My body aches all over, but I can do it. Adile and Gulnar are at my side as I make it down the stairs to my cutting table. Little Boss seems to not want much to do with me, but with as much haughtiness as she can affect she brings me material, scissors, and a pattern.

I'm a bit unsteady. Very slow . . . glad I'm not being hit. I have no other speed.

My body feels strange. I must try to eat. I'll feel better . . . then Ushi will throw me in the shower. Clean me up. And then . . .

I hear the clack of feet. Maybe the scissors weren't moving at all. I wait for the rod. It doesn't come. I look up. It's Ushi. Coming for me. She and Little Boss. They've come to get me, throw me into the shower. I smile. Am I not a prize even now? If only Ushi knew I'm still a virgin. That I'm really worth so much more than she assumes. I'm unclean, but I still have something special to offer.

They stop a short distance away. I can't keep from staring at Ushi.

"I don't want another one dying on us," I hear Ushi say as she turns and walks away.

Little Boss comes to my table and begins removing everything. "I'll take the scissors," she says, yanking them from my hand. "Go upstairs to your room."

"I don't want to," I say. I can't move. I won't. I don't know what this means.

"It's an order from Ushi. Just go," she says, and walks away.

My legs are shaking, but I understand only too well the hopelessness of defying Ushi. I weave as I begin my slow progress. A pair of small, strong hands supports me. It's Jemile, whose cutting table is nearby.

Too quickly a pair of large hands pulls her away. "I don't care if she has to crawl. You have your work to do. Get back there," Little Boss orders.

For a moment my eyes meet Jemile's. I'm glad that compassion has always been a strong part of our Uyghur hearts.

———

It is easy to find sleep, and I lose track of days and nights. I try to swallow water when forced to. Food is too difficult.

The factory is at last closed for its one-day break between orders. I'm left alone, although someone always seems to be here when I wake up. Perhaps the girls take turns. I'm glad they're allowed to go out. Their voices sound happy when they return. "Everything outside is lush and green," someone tells me.

"We've brought a gift," Gulnar says. "We met Chen

when we were taken to the town by one of the workmen and told him you were ill. He got something for us to bring to you. Something to eat. I've taken the pit out."

I press against the wall. I don't want food. I don't open my mouth. Everyone stands around watching as Gulnar forces a date into my mouth. Memories overwhelm me. The sweet, juicy flesh. The taste of Hotan. Thoughts of Mikray.

I lick my dry, cracked lips. "We must all have some to remind us of home," I say in a voice that's cracked too. One I hardly recognize as my own.

"No," comes a flood of responses. "They're all for you. If you eat them, it will make us happy."

"You eat them all, Roshen," Gulnar says. "I know where to go to get more." She bends over me, cradles my head. "And where to get help if we need it," she whispers as she puts another date into my mouth. I suck on it as I am given a round of applause. But I can't eat more. Not tonight. I give Gulnar's arm a squeeze and close my eyes. The room becomes quiet.

———

For a day I enjoy my diet of dates. I try to think it will make me well again. I'll show Ushi. I'll be back downstairs in no time. And then . . . again . . . I wonder if I want to be.

I go back to sleep.

Thirty-Nine

AND THEN I have a dream.

    A man's arms are around me.

    I struggle. Try to break free.

    Lash out with all my might.

    Until a smell surrounds me.

    A smell I know.

    And love.

———

It's Father. I am having a dream.

    A beautiful dream.

    "Try to walk, Roshen," he tells me.

    Somehow I do.

    I go with him.

    I think this may be paradise.

WE'RE FLYING IN the sky, high above the clouds. My head rests on Father's shoulder, but I try to stay awake to see what new visions appear in the small window at my side. Father asks me to sip from a container he holds in his hand, and I want to. I try to. The drink tastes special, like something Mother might have made from flowers that grow on bushes, and roots from deep in the earth.

It seems so real.

"What is happening?" I ask Father.

His hand covers my lips.

"Later," he says. "We'll talk when we get home."

Home.

That is a word used in dreams.

Like the dream I am having now.

Forty-One

WE FALL FROM the sky.

"It's all right," Father says. "It's part of our journey."

His hand trembles almost as much as mine.

———

Uncle is here to help Father. We're to ride in his truck. I'll know the countryside. I'll finally know if this is real. But the movement, the beat of the tires—my eyelids shudder and close.

Forty-Two

I AWAKE WHEN I hear whispering. The silhouetted figures standing in the doorway bring shivers of joy. "Come," I say. They rush in and enfold me in their arms. "Is it you, Mother? Aygul, is it really you?" These are the words I think. I try to say them, and maybe I do. My mother and sister do not answer. They rock me back and forth and cover me with tears.

For a long time we stay, holding, comforting. Then Mother leaves and comes back with a special drink. I swallow. Swallow again. She puts it aside. Aygul and I nestle against our mother.

"We're not home, are we?" I say. The room is dark, but it seems unfamiliar. I'm not lying on my own sleeping platform.

"We are not at the farm," Mother says. She strokes my forehead. "But you are with us, Roshen, and it is a time for you to eat and to get well. Will you do that for us?"

I don't answer.

"Let's try," Mother says. "Warm some of the broth we made, Aygul."

Mother helps me to sit up, holds me. Aygul brings a spoonful of broth to my mouth, which I open like a dutiful child. The taste brings memories of food fresh from our garden. It also brings a remembrance of half-rotten potatoes in slimy, bug-infested soup. My stomach churns. I think I might vomit. Aygul has another spoonful ready for me. I hold up my hand. I rub my stomach. Try to erase the horrible memory from my mind.

"There is no rush. Take all the time you need," Mother says.

For a while we sit in silence. I wonder if I will ever tell them what it was like. Their knowing would not change things.

My stomach settles. I take a few mouthfuls of broth before I become so heavy-eyed that Mother lowers me to the pillow.

"Sleep now, Roshen, but we will wake you every few hours to drink and eat." She tucks the blanket in, wraps me in a cocoon. "Grandmother, Aygul, or I will always be here beside you. You will never be alone."

———

They wake me and feed me. They bring pans and buckets of warm water and wash my hair. I begin to like my own smell again.

It's not too long before I find myself wanting to stay awake. "Will you draw the curtain back please, Mother? I'd like more light."

She opens the window, too, and I hear cicadas and birds.

"I'll leave you to the beautiful outdoor sounds for a moment," Mother says. "I'll be right back."

A lark's melody goes on and on. I lean back against a pile of cushions and blankets, content to listen to his music. With light coming through the window, I see more of the room. Books are stacked high on a chest along the wall. Another chest, much like mine at home, also stands against the wall. I think my eyes betray me; my mind still plays tricks.

I look out the window and try to spot the lark who is bringing me his wonderful song.

Suddenly his song stops. I hear hammering and the shrill whine of a power saw cutting through metal. I know these sounds. They're the sounds of Uncle's foundry.

"No," I cry in a voice too feeble to be heard as I turn away from the light—the truth—and sink into the pillows. Once again so weak I can't hold myself up. This is not the way my dream was meant to go.

Mother rushes into the room. Quickly closes the window. Draws the curtain. She comes to my side, rubs my brow, smoothes my hair.

I again find shelter in the darkness, and in Mother's familiar touch.

"Mother," I whisper, "why are we at Uncle's and not home on the farm?"

"Your father will tell you. He'll speak to you soon, now that you seem to be getting better," she says as she fluffs the pillows, tucks a blanket in around me, then heads for the door. "I must get back to the kitchen. I'll send Aygul in."

I shake my head no, but she does not see. I don't want to talk to Father. I want the curtain to stay drawn.

I close my eyes. Pretend to sleep, but Aygul pumps my arm. "Wake up," she says, and I try to shoo her away. "No, Roshen. It's Ahmat. He's here to see you. He comes every day, and Mother tells him it isn't time yet. But I thought you should know."

"Tell him I'm sleeping, Aygul. For I am."

Can you hear me, Ahmat?
I am here, yet I am not here.
I lie caged in a faraway land.
Perhaps one day I will waken and find my way home.

Forty-Three

ROSHEN," FATHER SAYS, "you must wake now. It's time for your tea. Your mother brought a fresh bowl. Can you drink it yourself, or shall I call her to help?"

My eyes blink open. There is only a soft light burning. I don't know how long I've slept or if it's day or night. I try to sit up, but my weakness has come back. "Call Mother, please," I say. Aygul holds me while Mother spoons the tea into my mouth.

"That's enough," I say after a few spoonfuls.

"You must finish it," Mother says. "You need the liquid, and it is your medicine."

I comply, and Mother and Aygul leave. I am left alone with Father.

He sits near me, on the rim of the sleeping platform. He does not take my hand or reach out to me. He sits quietly, as if in prayer, his hands clenched tightly in his lap.

"The new cadre came to see me, Roshen. He said someone from the factory had called him, told him you were deathly ill, that you would eat nothing and might die within days." Father unlocks his hands. His shoulders sag.

"If I offered to sell him the farm, the cadre would arrange for me to fly to Wuhan and have someone escort me to the factory so that I might bring you home. He would also settle all legal matters with the factory owner."

"No, Father!" I cry out, and the anger I've felt for months erupts inside me. I gasp for breath. I must tell him what happened, and I don't know how. Father puts his hands on my shoulders, tries to calm me. I shake him away.

"I made this happen," I say. "It's my fault." I look away as awful images of the fat man, Boss Lee, Ushi crowd my mind. "They wanted me . . . to . . ." My throat clogs. I can't speak these words to Father. "I starved myself to . . . to make myself ugly." My breath comes in short bursts as I struggle to control the words that scream in my mind. "It . . . it went beyond my control." My head is bowed. I see Father's hands, clasped in his lap, balled into angry fists. He understands what I'm saying. "I'm sorry, Father. I was a coward . . . and we lost the farm."

"Your life, Roshen, is not a sacrifice I'm willing to make." He stands and begins to pace, his feet heavy on the earthen floor. "It breaks my heart to think what you must have gone through." He stops in front of me. A bewildered look crosses his face. "They kept reporting how happy you all were, learning new skills, making new friends. They didn't let us contact you for fear it might make you more homesick."

He sits at my side again and takes my hands in his. "Listen, please, for a moment," he says, his voice now calm but full of sadness. "It was only a question of time before the cadre and his people took over our land. The government doesn't care that we loved our family heritage and could still make a good living from our farm. They have bigger plans, and they always get their way."

I want to pull away. But Father is so loving, so caring. So forgiving. Do I no longer know how to live in this world? I'm not the Roshen who left all those months ago.

Father tells more of the story. How Uncle needs him to help with the foundry. How the market for aluminum and steel pots is growing. He's invested money from the farm in Uncle's business. The government will likely leave them alone.

"I'm sorry, Father," I say. "I know you loved the farm and the life we led—I did too." Gently, I push his hands away. "I have to sleep now."

And then, again, I say I'm sorry.

I do not sleep. Had I chosen whoring, running away, or death, the farm would still have been taken from us. The idea that Ushi and Big Boss were instrumental in saving my life, that their action fell so perfectly into the hands of the cadre, appalls me.

I drag myself from my sleeping platform. Will my body to crawl hand over hand to the window. Yank at the curtain until it plunges to the floor. The window will no longer be covered. This world I live in is too real to be erased with the drawing of a curtain.

Forty-Four

I SIT AT A TABLE outdoors under the arbor, wrapped in a heavy blanket in spite of the spring weather. Mother helps me to come out here, tells me I look less like a skeleton than I did two weeks ago. She leaves food, a warm drink. She trusts me to be alone. I need to be.

I'm haunted by thoughts of my factory sisters. I didn't mean to abandon them. I only wanted to make myself ugly so Boss Lee would have no interest in taking me to his club again.

I pull the blanket tightly around me. Memories of the winter chill are more real than the warmth of the day.

I pick up my pen and open my notebook, and Mikray's voice comes to me: *Someday you'll turn our stories into poems for all the world to know.* I can almost see her saying this, her forehead tight, her eyes boring into mine.

I'm doing it, Mikray. Word by word, scratched out, tried again and again. Words to be heard by our Uyghur people and by the Chinese as well. The Chinese seem to be afraid of words, and I know some they may not want to hear about us factory girls—young girls ripped from their homeland and treated as slaves. No one I know of writes about us.

I'll tell the truth about the villainy that turned Hawa into a whore. About unpaid work and grueling hours, humiliations and cruelties and death. My poems will tell the story of Mikray, Gulnar, Jemile—all those whose fate I may never know. Of Zuwida, who lies forever in a foreign grave.

Will I ever be as brave as you, Mikray? Brave enough to send my poems into the secret network of our people—so they will be told behind closed doors and become the whispers that rouse my sisters to action?

Maybe I can do that. *Be sweet,* you said. I have no sweetness left, but I'll go to school, teach by day, and seem content. If I'm discovered, the Chinese will silence me. But I can't have voices shouting inside me and do nothing. Men build armies to rise against those who treat them badly. I must learn to make my words as powerful as an army.

I smile now. *What is it about you, Mikray, that makes me do things I would never have dreamed of?* I push aside the blanket I'm wrapped in. I stand. Take tiny steps. Take a few more. I will get strong. I take a deep, full breath and see Mother hurrying toward me.

"You have a visitor. It's Meryam."

I can never again live in the world of my childhood. I'm not much older than when I left, but my youth has passed. I care for Meryam. I should ask about her married life. Perhaps, too, I'm ready to find out about her brother. When Aygul or Mother mentions Ahmat's name, I shush them.

"I'd like to see her, Mother," I say.

Meryam bounces out the door, her steps like a dance. I know she's happy.

She stops. Bites at her lip to gain control. She's seen me —this person whose reflection even I don't recognize.

"It's all right, Meryam. Really. I'm so glad you've come."

The hug she was ready to give becomes a gentle holding of my hands. "Oh, Roshen, I didn't know," she says. "It must have been so awful."

We look away from each other, but our hands stay clasped.

"You were lucky not to be chosen. It would have changed your life in ways . . . that would not have been good." That's all I say, for I'm suddenly exhausted, not by the words but by the emotions that overwhelm me.

When Mother comes out with tea, she sees that I'm struggling. She stays to talk with Meryam. We find out that life at the silk maker's compound very much agrees with her. She's quite good at spooling silk threads, and she's learning to get along with her mother-in-law.

Mother picks up the empty tea bowls and prepares to leave. "It's time for Roshen to rest," she says.

"Oh, please, not quite yet. I need to be with Roshen for one more minute," Meryam says.

I'm not certain I want her to stay. If she has been sent as messenger, I know now that I'm not ready to hear about her brother.

She crouches next to me. "Please meet with Ahmat," she pleads. "I'm worried about him. He's a . . ." She stops. Leans in closer. "He's a protester. He hates what the Chinese are doing to us, wants the Uyghurs to have their own voice. He promises he won't go to rallies, but I don't trust him. The gatherings are meant to be peaceful, but the police don't always care. If he gets caught they'll send him away—or kill him. He must be careful. Maybe he'll listen to you."

I must have nodded, or made some gesture of compliance, for Meryam returns to her chair while I struggle to take in what she's told me.

"Ahmat sent you a gift, Roshen." She takes a package from her bag, places it on the table, and it's as if the whole world stands still for a moment. I'm in the toilet room throwing away the black ruffled blouse, the panty-showing skirt, the lace stockings—and the jade necklace. Ahmat's jade necklace. The most treasured gift I've ever received. Defiled by a pig. Thrown into the garbage.

My head drops to the table. I haven't the will or the energy to sit up. Meryam's hands tremble as she tries to comfort me. "He loves you, Roshen. When you first came home, he was here every day to see how you were. To see what he could do for you. Your family told him it was not yet time for him to see you. I know now that they were right, that you need time to heal. He's sent something he thought you'd like. Please let me tell him you still care."

My heart is full to bursting, that he cares so much. That I care so much!

When my breath comes back and I can once again speak, I say, "Tell Ahmat that I have deep feelings for him in my heart. Only . . ." I break off. There's so much I must tell him. Will he understand? "You see . . . he does not know the person I am now."

I try to get up from my chair, but I can't. "Please call Mother."

I clutch Ahmat's package to my breast as Mother and Meryam help me back to my sleeping platform.

Forty-Five

✦

I SIT UNDER THE ARBOR. Ahmat's gift, still un-
opened, is on the table. It's wrapped in plain paper and
twine. I think he has done this himself. Meryam would
have made it fancier.

I'm ready to open it. I untie the twine, remove the
wrapping.

There is a note inside.

> *Dear Roshen,*
>
> *Water flowing from the Kunlun; winds blowing from
> the desert. These words need no longer be codes between us.
> Thankfully, they are again a reality to us both.*
>
> *Having you nearby is a great comfort to me. I await your
> word of when we might see each other. Know, however,
> that I wait with impatience, but with respect.*
>
> *My deepest love,*
>
> *Ahmat*
>
> *P.S. There is much to talk about.*

When I can gather my emotions, I read the last line
again. *There is much to talk about.*

"Yes, Ahmat, there is," I say out loud. It seems we have
each journeyed to a new place. The naiveté of our first love

is over—as beautiful and innocent as it was, it is gone. I can never again offer him the purity of my body and mind. But I can offer him a friendship with a much deeper understanding. Together, perhaps, we can make a difference to our people.

I look at my gift. It is a pen and a sheaf of rare handmade mulberry paper. The tears that so easily flood my eyes these days flow down my cheeks. Ahmat has been told that I sit out here day after day with my pen and notebook. He believes I can write words worthy of being put on this precious paper. And I will!

I will not sign my poems. I can't if I want to stay out of jail and help my people. My signature will be the mulberry paper that carries my words.

I sit quietly. Strangely at peace. I place a sheet of the paper and the pen before me.

> *Dear Ahmat,*
> *It is time for us to meet. Time for a new reality for both*
> *of us, which may, or may not, take us down the same path.*
> *I am no longer afraid to find out.*
> *My deepest love,*
> *Roshen*

My mind is at rest. I close my eyes and listen for the songs of the birds. I hear the high-pitched twitter of a wagtail, and the thud of a hammer hitting metal, and the screech of a buzz saw cutting through iron—and my heart beats too fast. I can't get enough air.

The strikes of the hammer turn into the *thud, thud, thud* of Mikray's rivet machine; the whine of the buzz saw becomes the relentless whir of sewing.

I'm dizzy. Cold. So cold. I pull the blanket Mother has left for me around my shoulders and let my head sink to the table. Behind closed eyelids I see my sisters: Mikray, Hawa, Gulnar, Adile, Jemile, Patime, Letipe, Nadia, Nurbiya, Rayida, Zuwida.

I open my eyes and reach for a sheet of the mulberry paper, and my pen.

Afterword

In 2004, implementing what was called the Transferring Surplus Labor Force to Inner China policy, the Chinese government began to focus on using Uyghurs to fill their work-force quotas. Village officials sought out vulnerable Uyghur families and identified them to government officials. At the age of sixteen, many Uyghur daughters were sent from their rural homeland to work in factories located in Chinese cities.

Sending young girls far away from their homes is unthinkable in traditional Uyghur families. Uyghur parents hated the idea of their daughters living in a remote, hostile place where their culture would be suppressed, but they were forced to comply or face harsh punishment.

Radio Free Asia (RFA) gave this policy and the stories of Uyghur factory girls extensive coverage. Uyghur blog sites posted eyewitness accounts of Uyghur girls who became victims of sex slavery and organ trafficking rings. As a news organization, RFA was not able to confirm these accounts, since getting information on this kind of topic out of China is almost impossible. It is strictly controlled by the government.

In *Factory Girl*, Uyghur girls' experience in a Chinese factory where they and their workmates live under the scrutiny of local Chinese cadres is realistically conveyed through Roshen's touching story. Working conditions in the factory, the cultural and religious antipathy and hardship country girls face in big cities, the lure of material temptation, and exposure to corrupt dark corners in Chinese society are depicted in *Factory Girl* as if the author herself lived through all of these ordeals.

China continues to send young Uyghur women to coastal cities. Uyghurs must remain silent, as expressing their grievances would have dangerous—even fatal—consequences. It's sad to say, but many Roshens will face the challenge of being uprooted to strange cities and trapped in sweatshops.

Factory Girl gives voice to these young women in all their struggles and heroism, just as Roshen plans to do at the end of her story. It will open readers' eyes to a startling reality that exists in the world they live in today. I hope it will open their hearts as well.

Mamatjan Juma
Senior Editor, Uyghur Service
Radio Free Asia

Author's Note

Factory Girl is the story of Roshen, a Uyghur Muslim, who is taken from her home in the countryside near Hotan, China, and sent to work in a factory thousands of miles away. Although the novel is fiction, it is based on personal accounts I heard while traveling in Hotan and stories told to me by Uyghurs now living in the United States, as well as news reports and information gathered by human rights groups.

Uyghurs are ethnically and culturally a Turkic people living in an area they have inhabited for almost four thousand years. The land they call East Turkestan is now controlled by the People's Republic of China. The Uyghur people used to be ninety percent of the population of their homeland; the Han Chinese are now in the majority.

China's control of the Uyghur homeland has gradually evolved into suppression of the Uyghurs' unique culture and Muslim religion. When I traveled in the countryside around Hotan more than a decade ago, visiting the homes of craftsmen in nearby townships, a policeman stopped the car and demanded our group go to the station for questioning.

Our Uyghur guide convinced the officer we were harmless, and we continued on our way. This was alarming, but I didn't feel it was dangerous—more like a routine security check at the airport. There have been changes since then. Today, armored tanks are parked on the streets of Hotan; police patrol with guns.

Throughout China, Uyghurs are regarded with suspicion and contempt. The dire consequences that threaten Roshen and Mikray in the story are not exaggerated. Chinese authorities rule with a particularly heavy hand in the Muslim Uyghur homeland.

Government workers check identification papers of Uyghur worshippers as they enter mosques for Friday prayers. It is a crime to teach religion to children.

Children bearing such Muslim names as Arafat, Asadulla, and Mujahid for males and Amanet, Muslime, and Fatima for females are not allowed to attend school.

The Uyghur language has been severely limited or removed entirely from the education system. Proficiency in Mandarin, the official language in mainland China, is a requirement for employment.

Police search private homes to stop Uyghur gatherings and to seize weapons. Owning any printed material believed to be critical of the government is punishable by arrest and imprisonment.

Local officials monitor Uyghurs' cell phones and computers to spot "extremist" activities. Offenders are sent to "education" camps. Service for nineteen social media platforms in the Hotan area has been shut down by the government.

Any voice of dissent in East Turkestan has effectively been silenced. Unlike the people of Tibet, who receive a great deal of coverage in the world press, the Uyghurs and their plight are known to very few. More information about the Uyghurs can be found at uyghuramerican.org (current events and history); uyghurensemble.co.uk (music, literature, and history); josannelavalley.com (author information and photos).

It is my hope that the Uyghur people can maintain their unique identity and that someday they will see a better future for their homeland.